His DUCHESS

LUCINDA BRANT BOOKS

— Roxton Foundation Series —
NOBLE SATYR
HIS DUCHESS
HER DUKE
THEIR GRACES

— Roxton Family Saga —
NOBLE SATYR
MIDNIGHT MARRIAGE
AUTUMN DUCHESS
DAIR DEVIL
PROUD MARY
SATYR'S SON
ETERNALLY YOURS
FOREVER REMAIN

— Alec Halsey Mysteries —
DEADLY ENGAGEMENT
DEADLY AFFAIR
DEADLY PERIL
DEADLY KIN
DEADLY DESIRE

— Salt Hendon Books —
SALT BRIDE
SALT REDUX

A *New York Times*, *USA Today*, *Amazon*, and *Audible* bestselling author of award-winning Georgian historical romances and mysteries, Lucinda's books are renowned for their wit, heart-felt drama and a happily ever-after. She has degrees in history and political science from the Australian National University and a postgraduate degree in education from Bond University, where she was awarded the Frank Surman Medal. *Noble Satyr*, Lucinda's first novel, was awarded the $10,000 *Random House/-Woman's Day* Romantic Fiction Prize, and she has twice been a finalist for the Romance Writers' of Australia Romantic Book of the Year. Her novels have garnered multiple awards and become worldwide genre bestsellers. Lucinda lives a stone's throw from the beach, in a writing hut with wall-to-wall books on all aspects of the Eighteenth Century, collected over 40 years—Heaven. She loves to hear from readers (and she'll write back!).

lucindabrant@gmail.com | lucindabrant.com

pinterest.com/lucindabrant | twitter.com/lucindabrant

facebook.com/lucindabrantbooks | youtube.com/lucindabrantauthor

His DUCHESS

SEQUEL TO NOBLE SATYR

ROXTON FOUNDATION SERIES BOOK TWO

Lucinda Brant

A Sprigleaf Book
Published by Sprigleaf Pty. Ltd.

This is a work of fiction; names, characters, places, and incidents
are the product of the author's imagination or are used fictitiously.
Resemblance to persons, businesses, companies, events,
or locales, past or present, is entirely coincidental.

His Duchess: Sequel to *Noble Satyr*.
Roxton Foundation Series, Book 2.
Copyright © 2023 Lucinda Brant, all rights reserved.
Editing: Martha Stites and Cathie Maud Cabot.
Art & design: Sprigleaf.
Cover art reference: *Madame Charles Mitoire, née Christine-Geneviève
Bron with her children, nursing one of them* by Adélaïde Labille-Guiard.
Back cover 'postcard' crop art: *A Stag Hunt at Versailles* attributed
to Jean-Baptiste Martin.
Sedan Chair fleuron design by Sprigleaf.

Typeset in Adobe Garamond Pro.

Also in ebook, audiobook, and other languages.

ISBN 978-1-922985-55-2

10 9 8 7 6 5 4 3 2 1 Casebound Library Edition   (ii) I

for
Fiona

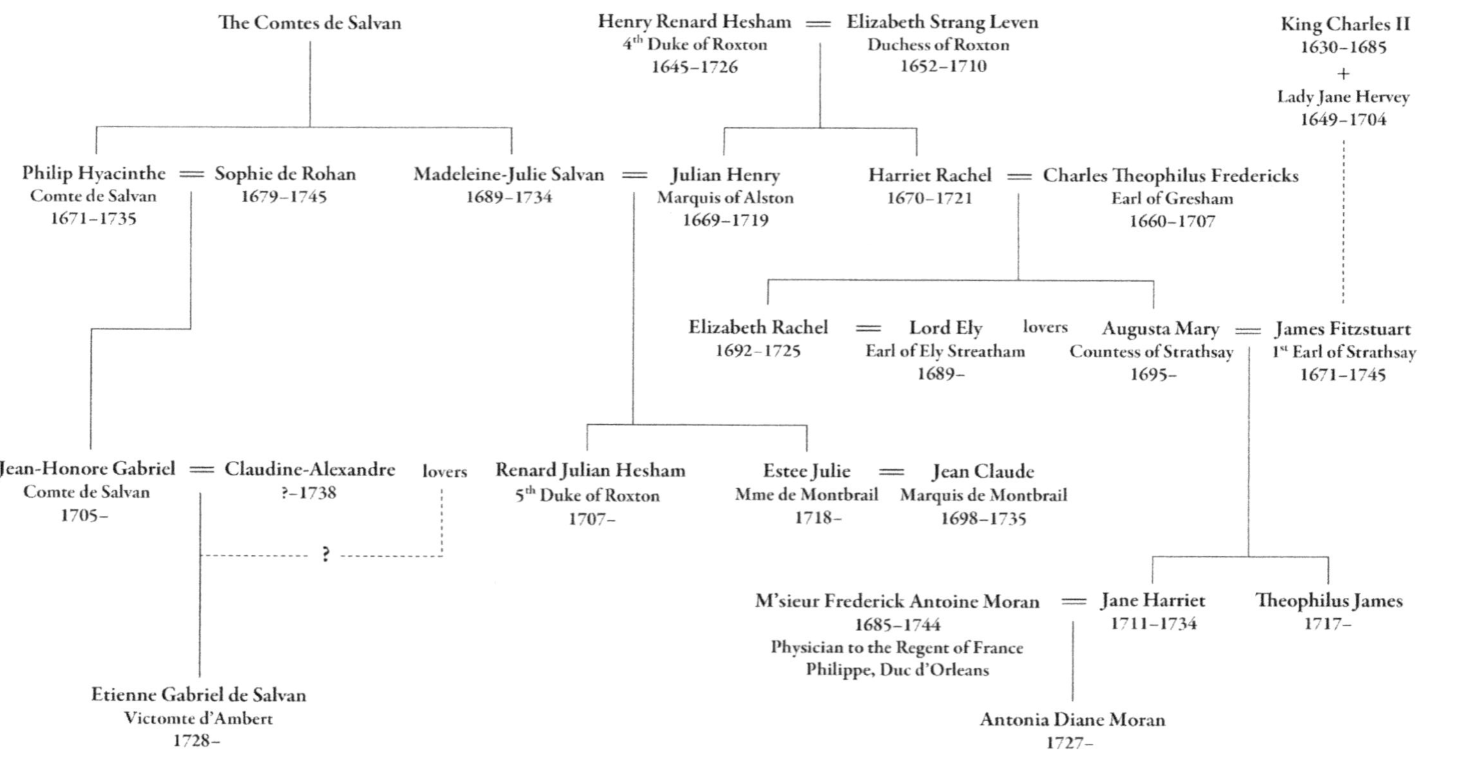

The Comtes de Salvan

Henry Renard Hesham = Elizabeth Strang Leven
4th Duke of Roxton   Duchess of Roxton
1645–1726   1652–1710

King Charles II
1630–1685
+
Lady Jane Hervey
1649–1704

Philip Hyacinthe = Sophie de Rohan
Comte de Salvan   1679–1745
1671–1735

Madeleine-Julie Salvan = Julian Henry
1689–1734   Marquis of Alston
                         1669–1719

Harriet Rachel = Charles Theophilus Fredericks
1670–1721   Earl of Gresham
                 1660–1707

Elizabeth Rachel = Lord Ely   lovers   Augusta Mary = James Fitzstuart
1692–1725   Earl of Ely Streatham   Countess of Strathsay   1st Earl of Strathsay
                   1689–   1695–   1671–1745

Jean-Honore Gabriel = Claudine-Alexandre   lovers
Comte de Salvan   ?–1738
1705–

Renard Julian Hesham
5th Duke of Roxton
1707–

Estee Julie = Jean Claude
Mme de Montbrail   Marquis de Montbrail
1718–   1698–1735

?

M'sieur Frederick Antoine Moran = Jane Harriet   Theophilus James
1685–1744   1711–1734   1717–
Physician to the Regent of France
Philippe, Duc d'Orleans

Etienne Gabriel de Salvan
Victomte d'Ambert
1728–

Antonia Diane Moran
1727–

DRAMATIS PERSONAE

The Roxton Family and household

Roxton—*Duke of Roxton aka M'sieur le Duc*

Antonia—*Duchess of Roxton aka Mme la Duchesse aka Comtesse du Roucy.*

Vallentine—*Lucian, Lord Vallentine, Roxton's best friend and married to his sister.*

Estée—*Lady Vallentine aka Madame, Vallentine's wife and Roxton's sister.*

Martin—*Martin Ellicott, Roxton's former valet and Julian's godfather (*mon parrain*).*

Julian—*Roxton and Antonia's infant son aka JuJu.*

Gabrielle—*Antonia's personal maid, youngest sister of Yvette, Rose, and Giselle.*

Céleste & Cécile—*infant Julian's wet nurses aka the Morvan* nourrices.

George Geraghty—*Roxton's valet.*

Jean-Luc Levron—*natural son of Roxton's father the Marquis of Alston and his mistress, a* marion-nettiste.

Augusta Fitzstuart—*the Countess of Strathsay aka* Grand-mère. *Antonia's grandmother.*

The Salvan Family and household

The ancient aunts—*sisters of Philip, Comte de Salvan. Roxton's aunts through his mother Madeleine-Julie; Salvan's aunts through his father Philip.*

Tante Philippe—*Marquise du Touraine-Brissac aka Mme Touraine-Brissac. Mother of Alphonse, Duc du Touraine. Grandmother of Elisabeth-Louise and Michelle Haudry.*

Tante Victoire—*the Comtesse du Chavigny.*

Tante Sophie-Adelaide—*twin sister of Victoire. A nun.*

Madeleine-Julie Salvan Hesham—*youngest of the Salvan sisters. Marquise of Alston, Roxton and Estée's mother d. 1734.*

Salvan—*Jean-Honoré Gabriel Salvan, Comte de Salvan. Son of Philip, Comte de Salvan, Roxton's first cousin. Nephew of the ancient aunts.*

Chevalier Montbelliard—*aka Cousin Hugh. The Comte de Salvan's heir.*

Michelle Haudry—*aka Mme Haudry, daughter-in-law of a Farmer General, daughter of Alphonse, Duc du Touraine, granddaughter of Philippe, Marquise du Touraine-Brissac.*

Alphonse—*Duc du Touraine, only son of Mme Touraine-Brissac, Roxton's first cousin and best friend. Father of Michelle Haudry and Elisabeth-Louise Salvan Gondi Touraine.*

Elisabeth-Louise—*sister of Michelle Haudry, granddaughter of Mme Touraine-Brissac.*

Thérèse—*Comtesse Duras-Valfons, Roxton's ex-mistress, wife of Baron Thesiger, sister of the Marquis de Chesnay, mother of the infant Robert.*

Gustave—*Marquis de Chesnay, Roxton's friend, brother of Thérèse Duras-Valfons.*

'Ricky'—*Richard Thesiger, Baron Thesiger, estranged husband of Thérèse Duras-Valfons.*

Giselle—*Elizabeth-Louise's personal maid, sister of Gabrielle.*

Historical figures appearing or mentioned

Louis—*King of France. Louis XV (1710–1774), known as Louis the Well-Beloved, King from 1 September 1715 until his death in 1774.*

Mme de Pompadour—*the King's* maîtresse-en-titre *(official chief mistress) aka Marquise de Pompadour, born Jeanne Antoinette Poisson (1721–1764).*

Comte d'Hozier—*the King's genealogist, keeper of* L'Armorial général de France *and* juge d'armes de France. *Louis Pierre d'Hozier (1685–1767).*

Marquis de Dreux-Brézé—Grand maître des cérémonies de France.

Joachim—*Marquis of Dreux-Brézé (1710-1781)*

Duc de Bouillon—*Grand Chambellan de France.*

Duc de Richelieu—*aka Armand, First Gentleman of the Bedchamber. Louis François Armand de Vignerot du Plessis (1696–1788).*

Marie Leszczyńska—*Queen of France (1703-1768), wife of King Louis XV.*

Marquis de Maurepas—*Minister of the King's Household. Jean-Frédéric Phélypeaux, Count of Maurepas (1701–1781) French statesman.*

M'sieur de Marville—*Lieutenant General of Police for Paris.*

ONE

VERSAILLES, FRANCE. LATE OCTOBER 1746.

"Here we are, doing what we do best. Sippin' your fine brandy by the fireside. Almost feels like old times, don't it?"

"It feels, my dear Vallentine, as it always does. Little has changed."

"Little?" Lord Vallentine gave a start. He never failed to take the bait. "How can you say that? It's a year to the day since you brought the chit into our lives, and if anyone had predicted this outcome, I'd have questioned their sanity!"

"As I frequently do yours...?"

"Ha! Ha! Stab me in the eye with a quill for pointin' out the obvious, but *that*—" He waggled a lace-covered wrist, finger extended to the right of his best friend's chair. "—*that* wasn't there a year ago, now was it?"

The Duke of Roxton appeared not to comprehend. "We were not in this house a year ago."

"Call this a house?" Vallentine gave a snort. "Damme! This ain't a house. It's a dog box!"

"I shall pass on your—er—*compliments* to Mme la Duchesse."

"No! No! Don't do that! She'll never let me hear the end of it." He peered closely at the Duke. "She chose this abode then, did she?"

"From the half dozen on offer."

"Well then, I'll reserve judgment until tomorrow mornin'. I did arrive in the dead of night. To be fair, all I've seen is the impressive *porte-cochère*, the enchanting entrance foyer, and the inside of this-this—what others would be content to call a library, but which is about as large as your closet back at the hotel. So that's not much to go on, is it?"

"No doubt in the daylight you will find it as charmingly pretty and as—er—*conveniently situated* for our purposes as does Mme la Duchesse."

"Charmingly pretty, you say? And-and—*convenient*? Ah. Yes. A'course it is!" Vallentine crossed his long, booted legs at the ankles and lifted his brandy tumbler. "Appreciate the forewarning."

The Duke inclined his head.

"You never did say why you've decamped to this charmin' and—um—conveniently situated villa," Vallentine persisted. "It's not as if you can't drive out from the hotel to Versailles whenever you please. And as it's only fourteen miles from hither to dither, your carriage-and-six can do it comfortably in half the time it takes the rest of us."

"An excellent question. Suffice that this quaint villa is expedient. It is close enough to the chateau for a sedan chair, but far away enough to be private. And not only does the walled garden gate give access to the royal park, so too does the stable courtyard. That makes its position well-suited to present—er—requirements."

Vallentine thought about this for a moment, then asked, "Has taking up residence here got anythin' to do with your duchess's presentation at Court?"

"It does."

"And she can't make her presentation at Court while still livin' at home in Paris?"

"I had assumed Estée had explained to you court etiquette and the—er—process of being presented to Their Majesties, so I need not."

"She did, but it didn't make much sense. All I can recall is that there's a public ceremony with lots of bowin' and scrapin' and snivelry and such, and in front of a pack of Court toadies. And once that's over with, your duchess will be officially permitted to careen about the private palace apartments with the rest of the fortunate few, such as yourself."

"Something like that," muttered the Duke.

"But I'm still mystified. It don't explain why you need to squeeze your household into this villa of your wife's choosin'. You've always come and gone from your Paris abode to spend time in Louis' company, and it didn't require you to live a stone's throw from his *chaise percée*. But if it's all because of your duchess's Court presentation, then I suppose needs must."

"There is no mystery, and you have answered your own question."

"I have?" When the Duke made no further comment, Vallentine shrugged and sighed and sipped at his brandy. After a pause he said, "If this is what your duchess wants, and you ain't too inconvenienced, then it's fine by me."

"Having your blessing, we can now sleep soundly at night."

Vallentine grinned. "I'll wager you haven't had a decent night's sleep in months!"

"I assure you, my dear, that when I do sleep, I sleep as I always have—as one dead."

Vallentine lifted his square chin and stared past the Duke's right shoulder. "You can tell me the truth, y'know. Antonia don't need to know."

The Duke blinked. "I did. And I keep no secrets from my wife, however trivial."

"Have it your way! But if you ask me, you bein' here has everythin' to do with what's by your chair." His finger was again stabbing the air in his friend's direction.

The Duke looked over his left shoulder at the floor-to-ceiling bookcase, then back at his best friend. "My books?"

"No! No! Damme! Not your books!"

"The fittings and the—er—fixtures mayhap?"

Vallentine swatted a hand in frustration. "Stop with the niggling, Roxton! You know very well I'm not referrin' to your possessions, or this house, but to the cherished occupant of that wicker thing—*thingum*."

"It's called a cradle, Lucian."

"That's it! A cradle! Y'think I'd know by now, what with 'em litterin' the hotel. Got one in every room here too, I don't doubt."

"Living as we are in a—er—dog box, fewer are required. But you are right," the Duke added quietly, gaze dropping to the cradle beside his chair. Its tiny sleeping occupant was tucked up between soft white linen sheets and a shell-pink quilted silk coverlet padded with goose feathers. "We are here so that he can be with us."

"I knew it!" Vallentine announced with satisfaction. "Estée said so. Not that she understands why you've had to move house. She said you could've left your heir in the care of his attendants while you and the Duchess were at Court. That's the usual thing to do."

"That was mooted. But you should know by now that where Antonia is concerned, nothing is usual."

"Ain't that the truth!"

"She would not entertain a separation from our son for the long hours required to be at Court," the Duke continued smoothly, as if His Lordship had not interrupted. "Taking up residence here means she can return whenever she feels the need. Children, particularly infants, are not permitted at Court—"

"What? No children at all in such a playground?"

"Whether born to the highest or lowest of court officials, infants are put out to nurse, and are rarely seen again until they are no longer children. They return when fully-formed adults. It is a—er—miracle of sorts."

"Surely the royal progeny ain't farmed out?"

"Naturally, they are the exception. But they are brought up well away from the public gaze. The only time I recall seeing the princesses was when returning from the hunt with His Majesty. He had the party wait while he stopped and spoke with his daughters. A few were still in leading strings. Now they are being educated—or as you inelegantly put it, farmed—er—out at the abbey at Fonevrault, well away from Court and its intrigues." A deep crease appeared between the Duke's black brows. "That is my first and last memory of children at the palace."

"Not surprisin' is it? Those gilded hallways aren't exactly a fit place for children of any age! Best they're not underfoot, or half the courtiers would be trippin' over cradles and such that the infantry require for their upkeep."

The Duke's gaze briefly returned to his sleeping son. He let out a breath. "I confess I had little understanding as to the amount of —er—paraphernalia required for the upkeep of one tiny being."

"Me neither, but I'm beginnin' to form a clearer picture. Estée isn't due for months, and already I'm trippin' over a mountain of this so-called *paraphernalia*. Damme!"

Roxton regarded his best friend with a wry smile.

"Infant and uncle alike. You've arrived here with enough baggage to take up occupancy."

"I thought you wouldn't mind if I stayed on for a few days after the chit's birthday celebration—oh, all right!" he admitted when the Duke showed mild surprise. "I've come to stay for a few weeks. Estée will let me know when I'm-I'm—"

"—permitted to return?"

Vallentine was sheepish. "Her physician tells me mornin' sickness is usual for the first few months."

"You only have yourself to blame, my dear."

Vallentine blushed. "When you put it like that, yes. But I didn't wish sickness upon her—or me!"

"No, you did not. Stay as long as you wish. Though I cannot promise that under this roof life will be any less—er—turbulent."

"Much obliged. I'll take turbulence over tantrums any day!" Vallentine declared, buoyancy returning. But to cover his slip in divulging more than he intended about the state of domestic disharmony within his marriage he quickly added, "Speakin' of infants bein' rarely seen, any particular reason why we are in the presence of your heir at this late hour?"

"My dear Vallentine, *he* is in *my* presence."

His friend grinned and shook his head. "I'll wager you'll never let him forget it, either!"

Roxton tugged at the large upturned cuff of his Chinoiserie silk banyan. His dark eyes sparkled. "I have great expectations for my son's acuity, that I will never need to remind him."

"Can you doubt it when you're his sire?" Vallentine leaned forward to peer into the wicker cradle, and lowered his voice as if he'd just remembered he was in the company of a slumbering infant. "It's difficult to tell, what with him wearing that fetching cap, but I presume he's still got a full head of black hair?"

"He does."

"Grown much?"

"Since you saw him a fortnight ago? Of course. He grows every day. That's what infants do best."

"And cry!" Vallentine squirmed on his seat and pulled a face. "They do that *a lot.*"

The Duke's mouth twitched. "My son does not cry, Lucian, he makes his demands known, as is his right."

"Ha! And that battalion of nursery maids that usually surrounds him comes running!"

"As they ought. Between them they have decades of experience dealing with infants. His mother and I have all of three months."

"That's three months more than me," Vallentine grumbled good-naturedly.

"I am counting the days until you join me in facing up to the full weight of responsibility that comes with fatherhood."

"I'll wager you are! Damme! But you can stop countin'. I'm already gettin' a daily earful of what is expected of me, and I can tell you I'm not confident I'll be able to live up to expectations."

"My advice is not to bother. You never will."

"Duly noted." Vallentine gave a huff of laughter and rolled his eyes. "Sisters! Wives!"

The Duke turned dark eyes upon his best friend that were as inscrutable as ever.

"Let me put you out of your misery, Lucian. I am well aware Estée has charged you with discovering, and then relaying to her post-haste, the arrangements in my son's nursery, all so she can write to Antonia with more unwanted advice. Antonia did not heed her—er—*interference* at the hotel, thus she is unlikely to do so here, merely because we have exchanged one residence for another. And before you start moving your jaw up and down without saying anything intelligible—because you have no wish to be disloyal to me, or to your wife, or to Antonia—let me assuage your worry. I do not hold you accountable for your wife's behavior. I know my sister well enough by now. More brandy?"

Vallentine stuck out his tumbler with a sigh of relief, but kept his eyes lowered to the amber fluid being poured from a crystal decanter. He then waited while the Duke ordered coffee from a liveried footman who came out of the shadows on his signal, before admitting with a guilty smile,

"Truth told, I'm glad you know what I was fishin' for, because Estée won't rest until I send her news."

"The birth of her own child cannot come soon enough. It will direct her energies where they are most appreciated. Though I blame myself—"

Vallentine gave a start. "You do?"

The Duke studied the large square-cut emerald on his ring finger, turning it into the candlelight and saying with uncharacteristic hesitancy, "Fatherhood has given me pause… and caused me to *reflect* upon my history."

"Not much you can do about that now," Vallentine interrupted with a snort into his brandy tumbler.

The Duke set his jaw. "Not *that* history," he hissed. "My *distant* past. When I was a boy and both my esteemed parents were still alive."

His gaze wandered to the fireplace. He did not see the glowing embers, but one of the many opulent drawing rooms in his Parisian mansion on the Rue Saint-Honoré. It was draped in blue velvet and silks, with white gilded furnishings and a *Savonnerie* floral carpet. It had been his mother's favorite room and where he had spent the most time with his parents.

"When I think on it," he mused. "I now recognize that my father was an exemplary parent; I could ask for none better. Estée was deprived of having such a father."

"Hardly your fault."

"His untimely death wasn't *literally* my fault. But what came later… Once I succeeded my grandfather to the dukedom… Estée was still a child, young enough to need a father's guidance. I failed to provide her with that."

His Lordship sat up with a frown. "You can't beat yourself up over fate. You were, what—eleven or twelve—when your pater died? And I remember when the old Duke shuffled off this mortal coil, because it's not every day your best friend succeeds to a dukedom! We'd spent a long night in the cellars, helping ourselves to his considerable wine collection, when half a dozen of his most dour servants woke us up with the news. Damme! Never had such a thumpin' headache in all my days! You were eighteen or nineteen—"

"Nineteen."

"*Nineteen*. Who knows anythin' about parentin' at that age? Who wants to!?"

"I could not have said it better myself."

Vallentine shook his head and gave a huff of laughter. "And if we're bein' frank, at that age you certainly weren't fit to be a parent, to Estée or anyone else. And who could blame you? You had enough on your plate balancin' that ducal coronet on your young head and worryin' about your new-found responsibilities. I remember. You said you felt like chuckin' the thing in the Thames, and all the toadies and catch farts could go hang!"

Roxton met his best friend's blue eyes as his hand dropped to the cradle beside his wing chair. He took to rocking it gently to and fro; his son had begun to fuss. "Hold to that memory and the inexperience of youth when you write to Estée about your visit here with us."

Vallentine's gaze darted to the wicker cradle and then back up to the Duke. His eyes widened on a sudden thought. "You don't think… I wasn't referrin' to-to your duchess when I said—damme, Roxton! What I said about bein' too young and not knowin' the first thing about bein' a parent was about *you* at nineteen. I wasn't takin' a swipe at Antonia—"

"And yet how apposite. Or so Estée would say…"

Vallentine lost his smile and pulled his square chin into the folds of his stock, not breaking eye contact with his noble brother-in-law. "Look. I know Estée hasn't been backward in comin' forward with her opinions about motherin' and infant feedin' and the like. To be honest, I only listen to one word in twenty because she might as well be speakin' Egyptian for all I know about newborns. So, despite me nigglin' you about why you've taken up residence in this villa, I'm not a complete dunderhead! You're here because you want to give Antonia some breathin' room from-from —all that well-meanin' *advice* my wife and others have been dishin' out to her."

"Estée's morning sickness arrived at a most opportune time. Providence intervened, saving me the bother."

"Point taken. But as your sister's husband, I'd like to think I know her well enough to say in her defence that her interferin' in your life—more to the point, Antonia's—has everythin' to do with her great love for you both and your infant. She's the way she is because she cares deeply. I'll grant she's highly strung, over-protective, and fiercely female to her fingertips, but there's no malice in her."

"I agree. And I don't think her malicious." The Duke sighed. "But Estée's—er—motherly *concern* has manifested itself into unwelcome interference, not only in how we choose to rear our son, but in all aspects of our lives. I am mindful, even if my sister is not, that Antonia became a mother while still a bride, which has left her little time to come to terms with, least of all enjoy, her position as my duchess."

Vallentine was about to make a glib response to lighten the mood about how the Duke might be feeling neglected now he had an heir demanding everyone's attention, Antonia's most of all, when he was diverted by the snuffling noises of an infant waking.

The Duke, too, was distracted. It took but one look across to the other side of the fireplace for two nursery attendants, dressed in customary dark gowns with white starched aprons and caps, to appear out of the shadows and at the edge of the circle of orange light. And when the Duke removed his hand from the cradle, one of the women scuttled forward to scoop up his little lordship before his distress grew louder and more insistent.

"Where is Mme la Duchesse?" Vallentine asked, watching the two women fuss and coo over the infant as they spirited him across the room to a chaise longue. "She don't usually let her son out of her sight."

"That was true at the hotel," the Duke replied getting to his feet, but not moving away from his chair. "Here, we are attempting a new—er—*regimen*."

His Lordship mechanically followed the Duke's lead. It was not the standing that surprised him most, but the fact his best friend did not answer him in English, but in French, the language he always used when the Duchess was present.

"Whatever this new regimen is," Vallentine commented with a huff, "you don't look convinced that it's workin'!"

"You asked as to Antonia's whereabouts. She should be sleeping soundly in our bed. Regrettably, she is not."

When the Duke turned to the wall of books perpendicular to the fireplace, Lord Vallentine did likewise. One of the bookcases was pushed outwards into the room. It was not a bookcase at all, but a door that concealed the entrance to a stairwell. The staircase connected the library with the main bedchamber above. Framed in the doorway holding an ornate silver chamberstick was the Duchess of Roxton.

TWO

Antonia came out of the small alcove of the stairwell in a whirlwind of soft lilac silk and white lace. A matching silk banyan was thrown over her nightgown and on her white-stockinged feet were a pair of matching lilac silk mules. A fat satin ribbon tied in a haphazard bow was doing its best but failing to keep her abundance of messy golden curls from falling about her shoulders to the small of her back.

"I did try to go back to sleep, Monseigneur," she confessed, putting aside the chamberstick and coming straight up to the Duke. She took hold of the hand he held out to her. "But when I woke and you were not there, I forgot we were not at the hotel. And when Julian's crib it was missing I—but none of that matters now! Vallentine, you are here," she said happily, turning a sleepy smile on her brother-in-law. "I am very pleased to see you, even if it is the middle of the night. But why were you not here yesterday, as I—"

"Roxton invited me for your birthday," Vallentine interrupted in a rush, cutting her off. Accompanying this uncharacteristic rudeness was a significant glare at her and then a swift, wary glance

at the Duke before he added, addressing them both, trying to
sound nonchalant, "What sort of brother-in-law would you take
me for if I hadn't accepted Roxton's invitation to the celebration,
eh? Got to help you enjoy the day. It's not every year you turn
nineteen."

Antonia returned his glare before rolling her eyes. "Why else
would you be here? And it is not every year. It is only *this* year."
She looked up at the Duke with a cheeky smile. "Monseigneur, I
had no idea Vallentine could count, did you?"

The Duke smiled down at his wife. "I am as surprised as you,
mignonne."

"Eh? What? Of course I can count to—Oh! Ha! Ha!"

Distracted by her son's whimpering, Antonia excused herself,
disappearing into the shadows. Vallentine considered it an opportune moment to turn in for the night, as the infant's cries were
growing more insistent. But in the next moment the crying
stopped, and the Duchess reappeared, all smiles.

"He is dry again and back on the breast." She leaned into the
Duke, adding confidentially with a frown of puzzlement, "Renard,
Céleste she is feeding him—*again*."

"Not unsurprising, or unreasonable," the Duke informed her.
"It has been almost three hours since he last demanded
sustenance."

"I slept for *three* hours?" Antonia asked in wonderment. "But
that is not possible!"

The Duke smiled, drawing her closer. "It is entirely possible.
You did not sleep at all well last night, because your son would not
settle."

"He is *my* son when he is most demanding," Antonia
complained without heat. "And *your* son when he is sleeping the
sleep of the angels!"

"Naturally." The Duke gently brushed a curl from her flushed
cheek. "*Ma vie*, I had hoped you would sleep through until
morning."

"But how was I to do that when you are here and not in bed with me? This regimen we have decided upon, it requires that we both adhere to it or it will not work, yes?"

The Duke played with her fingers. "I had every intention of keeping my part of the bargain, but there was an—er—impediment."

"Impediment?" Antonia caught her breath, green eyes widening and gaze darting in the direction of the shadows. "With Julian? What impediment?"

"Poor choice of word," the Duke apologized. "I was about to return to our bed when I was informed Lucian was on the doorstep with a mountain of baggage. So I played congenial host."

Antonia glanced at Vallentine. "Yes, I see that Vallentine he is one big impediment to you coming to bed but—"

"Hey!" Vallentine objected and pulled a face.

"—if you have Julian with you in the library, and not in the nursery with Céleste and Cécile, then we are no better off than we were at the hotel when his cradle it was in our bedchamber, yes?"

"Damme! She's got you there, Roxton!" Vallentine stuck in with a huff of laughter, and was ignored by the couple.

"I agree with you, *mignonne*," the Duke replied smoothly, "but do you not recall what we were advised this afternoon, about the Dutch heater in the nursery gallery?"

"I know I should remember but I do not," Antonia stated truthfully, plucking at the Duke's fingers. She sighed, adding forlornly, "I had such a good memory before Julian arrived, and now I wish more than ever it would return because there is so much in a day for me to remember..."

"The Dutch heater needed repair," continued the Duke, ignoring her self-castigation. "I'm told it takes at least a day for it to radiate enough warmth, particularly for such a space as the gallery. That was the impediment. The solution was to have Julian here in the library where it is warm."

Antonia's green eyes widened in understanding. "So he would be the floor below us—"

"—and only a secret stairwell away. Yes."

"Not very secret, is it," Vallentine quipped, "if we all know about it."

Antonia gave him a quizzical frown. "Sometimes I do not understand you, Vallentine. Just because it is called a secret stair does not make it so."

"Well you got that right," Vallentine mumbled, deflated.

"I am sorry," she added quickly, a heightened color to her cheeks and a hand to her brother-in-law's velvet sleeve. "I do not mean to be so-so *grincheuse*. I am tired. Tomorrow I will be myself again. But I will apologize also before I forget that there is every possibility you will be woken early by the noises made by small children. This is not the hotel, and so the rooms they are close and the walls thin. There is nothing for it but to tolerate it because, no matter the great honor done them to be the nurses of M'sieur le Duc's heir, I would not have Céleste and Cécile separated from their own babies so they can care for Julian."

"How many children are we talking about?" Vallentine asked with alarm.

Antonia shrugged and threw up a hand. "I do not recall. The number it is unimportant."

"Don't recall? *Unimportant?*" Vallentine was aghast. He glanced at the Duke, expecting him to comment. He did not. "If these females are experienced wet nurses by vocation, then it's my guess they've got at least half a dozen brats between them. And as their mammas will be occupied with your precious infant there is every possibility of their brats escapin' the nursery and runnin' amok through this house."

"Why do you worry about trivialities?" Antonia complained. "The only importance is M'sieur le Duc's son, and that he Julian be nursed by Morvan *nourrices* who are content and happy and without worry. Only in this way will they produce milk that is also happy and content, and so Julian he will be also. That is what I am told, and what I believe. And these women will be anything but happy if they do not have their own children with them. It is logical and reasonable. As logical and reasonable as the fact that little children they make noise. There will be no peace. But it cannot be helped. All that matters is Julian." She kissed the back of the Duke's hand then let it go. "You both must excuse me. I must see my son one last time before I return to bed."

"I did warn you about the turbulence," the Duke remarked to His Lordship without apology, not the least concerned, gaze remaining on Antonia as she swept across the room.

"No small wonder why you took a house with a garden gate that opens out onto the park," Vallentine whispered loudly. "You can have the gardener leave it wide, and hopefully the Morvan brats will escape, never to be seen again."

"Lucian, that gate is for our escape. The King's hunt passes this way, and tomorrow morning I will be joining it. You are welcome to join me...that is if you have no other—er—pressing engagements?"

The last sentence saw the Duke tear his gaze from Antonia to raise an eyebrow at his brother-in-law in expectation of a full confession. It came within seconds.

Under the Duke's unblinking gaze Vallentine was suddenly hot beneath his cravat. He gulped, and sidled up to him. Both returned to watching the Duchess, who was conversing with the wet nurse, while her infant son's attendants crowded closer in a semi-circle behind the chaise longue.

"You know, don't you?" Vallentine hissed, shoulder to shoulder with the Duke.

"What do I know?" Roxton asked in the same whispered aside.

"That I'm pathetic at subterfuge! That's what! Damme!"

"You are. But I fail to understand why you are telling me something I have known for years."

"Can't play a decent hand of cards for the same reason."

"You are woeful at cards. That's true."

"And you and Estée can read me like a book!"

"Again, this confessional is nothing new."

"Look here. I know you know me comin' here wasn't only to help the chit celebrate her birthday. I'd have to have gruel for brains not to realize by now that no matter is too insignificant to warrant your attention where your family is concerned. But truth is, I've not blurted it out to you because she made me promise to keep it to myself. I can't break a promise."

"Then you must not."

"What?"

"Break your promise."

"But-but—I have to tell you! You need to know what I—what she—what we—"

"All I need to know tonight is that if there were a possibility of danger—"

"*Danger?*" Vallentine was incredulous.

"—you would protect her."

"Let any scoundrel try to come within ten feet of her!"

"As I thought. And I have every confidence in your—er—sword arm."

"I'd protect her with my life. On my honor."

The Duke turned his head to look at his best friend. A wisp of emotion choked his voice. "I do know that. If any harm were to befall her, I-I—"

"Don't you worry. A man would have to be a Bedlam inmate to take on the greatest swordsman in all of France and England. That's me by the way."

The tension eased in the Duke's neck and his black eyes sparked. "Thank you for the reminder, Lucian."

"But between you and me, it ain't danger that's worryin' me. I don't think there is any, to be perfectly honest. It's keepin' a secret from you. I've never been good at keepin' anythin' from you, and I don't want to start now because—"

"No," the Duke interrupted. "You gave her your word. Keep it. Now you must excuse me. It has been a very long day." Antonia stood at the entrance to the secret stair waiting for him. But before going to her, and in a rare show of public emotion, the Duke briefly gripped then patted Lord Vallentine's velvet sleeve. "You are a fine man, Lucian." Adding with a crooked smile, "And I am an excellent judge of character. Good night, my dear."

"Hey! What about your coffee?" Vallentine called out as a footman came up carrying a heavy tray of coffee things.

"You enjoy it," the Duke replied without turning around.

Taking the hand his duchess held out to him, Roxton followed her into the secret stairwell and closed over the bookcase door.

⚶

ALONE AT LAST, all semblance of ducal decorum evaporated. He pulled her to him and she, with a giggle, threw her arms about his neck and pressed herself against him. They enjoyed a tender kiss in the confines of the darkened stairwell before he effortlessly swept her up off her feet and carried her the short flight of stairs to their opulent apartment above. Here there was warmth and light and every conceivable comfort. Two sleepy-eyed liveried footmen, who lingered at the far end of the *enfilade*, instantly made themselves scarce, disappearing behind a paneled door into a servant corridor. By the time the ducal couple reached their spacious bedchamber and the large canopied four-poster bed with its painted silk hangings, their clothing was strewn across the parquetry and deep carpets of three connecting rooms.

THREE

THE NEXT MORNING, at first light, the soft chiming of a clock woke the Duke from a heavy slumber. The chiming brought his valet into the bedchamber. Ellicott silently padded about, pulling back and securing the heavy damask curtains from a row of long windows with their view of the royal parkland. The undulating autumnal landscape was blanketed in low-lying mist, the dawn sky hovering between night and day, and the sun was but a thin bright line on the horizon. It all boded well for the King's hunt.

In the adjoining rooms there was plenty of activity for the start of a long day. One of two linen-lined copper bathtubs set before the fireplace was being filled with hot water. A riding ensemble of black velvet frockcoat, waistcoat, and knitted riding breeches, jockey boots, and matching black cravat were laid out in the dressing closet. And on the walnut dressing table, to one side of the shaving bowl and razors, a heavy silver tray had upon it a sparse breakfast. The silver chocolatier with its straight ivory handle and ornate hinged lid was set on a lamp stand, the heated oil keeping the contents at drinking temperature. And under a silver-domed lid stamped with the Roxton ducal coat of arms, on a Sèvres porcelain plate, were warm, soft bread rolls.

Every task and action was carried out with quiet exactitude by the male servants going about their duties in specially-made soft kid shoes that dulled noise on parquetry and made none on the carpets. Their liveried coats with the distinctive ducal R embroidered in silver over the right breast set them apart from the rest of the household servants, and gave them permission to come and go from their master's private apartments at will. The Duke's most trusted retinue, these men were highly trained, well-compensated for their discretion, proprietorial of their superior position, and utterly loyal. To gain the trust and earn the right to wear such distinctive livery, most had been employed in the Duke's household in lesser roles for at least five years. And when they were elevated to that of personal attendant in the ducal apartments, they had to quickly familiarize themselves with their master's routine, and not only anticipate his wants and needs, but never be seen unless seen first.

It was rare for the Duke to address any of these servants directly—he had no need to do so. All communication came through his valet. Whether it was his private apartments in Paris or London, or at his vast country estate of Treat in Hampshire, life remained as it had always been since the Duke came into the title at the age of nineteen. But then, a mere ten months ago, and in the prime of his life, His Grace married. Not so long after that—it seemed but a blink of an eye to some—the couple welcomed a son and heir.

And nothing in the ducal household had been the same since.

Before his marriage, the Duke had often started the day fatigued by ennui. He had certainly not woken with anticipation for what a new day might bring. He had presumed that such a heightened keenness for the unknown was only experienced by lame-brained optimists and very small children. He was a creature of habit, a taciturn disciple of order and obedience. Life revolved around him, conformed to his expectations, and his very existence set its particular pattern and rhythm. Anything less was an undignified chaos below what was expected of a duke, and not just any duke, but the Duke of Roxton, grandson of an English duke and a French comte, and an unbroken patrician lineage stretching back centuries.

And yet, since becoming a husband and a father, his world had tilted on its axis. There was continual disruption to the pattern of his days, its rhythm frenetic at best. He woke never knowing what the day would bring. The only constants he had were his household, which continued on as smoothly as the complicated mechanisms of one of a dozen of his beautiful timepieces, and the unconditional love and devotion of the woman who had not only captured his heart but turned his life on its end.

To a lesser man, to a more rigid mind, such monumental upheaval would not have been tolerated. To the fifth Duke of Roxton, his marriage had saved him, from boredom and an excruciating loneliness. He was the happiest he had ever been in his life. And it was all due to the bright, beauteous vortex of love and light with whom he now shared his life, and who he still could not quite believe was his duchess.

Every morning since his wedding day, whether he rose early or late, the moment he was awake he looked for her. Most times she was asleep beside him, golden honey hair in a mussed plait or a tangled cloud about her lovely form. And at those times he would curl around her fragrant loveliness and return to a blissful sleep. But if she were not with him, but in her bath or being dressed, or, more recently, preoccupied with their infant, he would not return to sleep but lie in the darkness, or the early morning light, and say a silent prayer of thanks to God for his good fortune. And in those first months of their marriage he had continued to wonder what he had done to deserve her and this life he was now leading with her, and now with the son and heir she had given him.

And then one day, not so very long ago—it was the morning

after the birth of his son—the answer struck him so forcibly that it was like a lightning bolt come out of a clear sky. He could only describe it as an epiphany. He no longer pondered what he had done to deserve the life he was now leading, but rather knew what he must do to ensure its continuance: It required that he live a life that was deserving of his wife and the family they would raise together. It would be a life of purpose, one that set the foundation for future generations, and one that nurtured those who were important in their lives.

As the premier duke of England and the wealthiest nobleman either side of the Channel, he had the power, the means, and the resources at his disposal, to put this new-found purpose into effect. It would mean further changes to his life, and he immediately set about making them, without the slightest hesitation.

Bringing his family to this villa close to Louis' chateau was just the beginning, and a small part of the larger plan. The first major change required the cooperation of his valet. And there was no time like the present to put his intentions into action.

So when Ellicott placed a silk banyan at the foot of the bed, and turned to leave, gaze never leaving the carpet, one softly-spoken word from the Duke was enough to freeze his movements on the spot, as the Duke knew it would. Rarely, if ever, had they exchanged a word in a bedchamber.

"Wait," the Duke hissed as he slid out of bed, careful not to disturb the covers and wake the Duchess. He shrugged the banyan over his nakedness, pulled the hair out of his eyes, and came up to his valet, who remained with his back to the bed and as still as a statue. "Follow," he whispered, and went on ahead, down the length of the *enfilade* in his bare feet until he was in his dressing room.

A LANGUID HAND waved at two startled attendants, who had not been expecting their master until after his bath, saw them scurry out of the dressing room, leaving the Duke alone with his valet.

Roxton went to the dressing table and flipped the lid on the *chocolatière* and inserted the wooden frothing stick. He then set to rubbing the stick between his palms so that it stirred the hot chocolate to a smooth, frothy consistency. And while he fastidiously prepared his morning beverage, he issued his instructions.

Martin Ellicott did not move a facial muscle.

"You are to return to Paris immediately. And be back tomorrow by noon. Take the carriage. And while you are at the hotel, find five minutes between tasks, or however you—er—manage such things, and call on the Lady Estée. Offer her my compliments and tell her we are all thinking of her in her time of distress, particularly her husband. She will accuse him of any number of false crimes, and call down the plagues of Egypt upon us all for abandoning her. I would be surprised if she does not offer up a long list of petulant ills we have caused her by our seeming—er—callousness in leaving her behind at the hotel. Naturally you will endure this outrage and her haranguing with your usual tact and acumen."

"Yes, Your Grace," Ellicott replied in English, for his master had spoken to him in the language of the old Duke, the only language that ancient nobleman had permitted his heir to speak while living under his roof. It put him on heightened alert for what was to come. The Duke only conversed with him in English when he had something of vital importance to tell him and wished no one else to know.

Roxton gently tapped the frothing stick on the lip of the *chocolatière* and set it aside on a saucer, a quick look up at his valet before returning to the task at hand. He carefully poured out the chocolate into a patterned porcelain mug.

"I am confident my sister will conclude her theatrics by waving a stack of correspondence under your nose," the Duke continued, taking a sip of the bitter-sweet brew. "Letters for Lord Vallentine, for me, and there will be several for Her Grace. Bring them all to me. The Duchess can do without my sister's ill-chosen homilies on the mothering of ducal heirs and the feeding and watering of noble infants. And these from a female who has yet to produce an infant of her own. Ye Gods!" He let out a breath of frustration and set the mug on its saucer. As he did so, his long black hair fell across his brow, momentarily hiding his face, and he said through his teeth, frustration getting the better of him, "I did not uproot my family from the ancestral pile and bring them here to this—er —*dog box* on a whim."

There followed a long pause, one Ellicott assumed was made so he could offer comment. That perhaps the Duke had delayed his preparation for the King's hunt and brought him here for the express purpose of seeking his advice, or at the very least, to provide a sounding board for his concerns regarding the Duchess and their infant. Since the Duke's marriage, Ellicott was no longer surprised by anything where his noble employer was concerned. And so he offered his opinion, said from the heart, and startled even himself with his candor.

"A wise decision, Your Grace. One I am confident will greatly benefit Her Grace and his little lordship. Her Grace is young, and as he is her first, there must be times when she is overwhelmed by the task of mothering. It cannot help that he has, by all accounts, an exceedingly voracious appetite for the breast. An excellent sign of his health and wellbeing to be sure, but one that, dare I say it, has added to the Duchess's burden. Hiring the Morvan wet nurses, and allowing them to bring their families into the nursery, was a stroke of genius. They will not only cater to his little lordship's increasing demands for nourishment, but also give Her Grace peace of mind. And, dare I add, provide you both with a welcome respite from the constant needs only an infant can demand."

It was rare for the Duke to be lost for words, but he was now. He pulled the hair out of his eyes and stared at his uncharacteristically loquacious valet with knitted black brows, as if wondering what had come over him. And for want of something to cover his mute astonishment he took another sip of hot chocolate. A sudden slight tremor in his hand made him set it down again.

Ellicott witnessed the tremor, saw the dark frown and startled expression, and interpreted this as a thunderous anger with him for voicing his opinion on a highly intimate topic that was not his to comment upon in any capacity. He doubted Lord Vallentine spoke so freely to the Duke. His face drained of color. He swayed. There was a buzzing in his ears. What had come over him?

But he knew who was to blame, and why, and she was sleeping three rooms away.

He and the Duke had known each other since they were boys and Ellicott had been his valet for almost two decades. And yet he had never spoken so openly to him as he had just now. He had lowered his guard to the point of crossing the invisible line that separated their disparate societal positions, all because he cared deeply. No. Care was not the right word. He loved him, and he had fallen in love with his duchess, too. To him they were his family. But what he had done just now, in his capacity as valet, was unprofessional, unconscionable, and unforgiveable. He must resign immediately. But first he must apologize. He must…

When the Duke spoke, it took a moment for Ellicott to come to his senses. And when he realized the Duke had addressed him by his Christian name his sigh of relief was audible.

"Dear me, Martin," the Duke drawled, raising one mobile eyebrow. "We have all allowed ourselves to fall under the spell of one tiny being, have we not? And you know better than anyone I am not referring to my son. No! Do not apologise for speaking your mind. As for speaking out of—er—turn, I will deal with that later. Tomorrow, in fact. Upon your return, come to the library."

"Yes, Your Grace," Ellicott replied evenly, heart still racing, cheeks flushed and gaze on the parquetry.

The Duke's lips twitched. "You can spend tonight and

tomorrow morning ruminating about what it is I wish to discuss with you. What I require from you now is to listen, and then be on your way. And I don't need to say this but I will: Not a word, to anyone, tiny or otherwise."

AN HOUR LATER, Martin Ellicott was the only occupant of the Duke of Roxton's magnificent carriage, trundling along the Versailles road to Paris. The ducal coat of arms on the black lacquered doors announced the owner's nobility, while the carriage's luxurious velvet and silk interior, modern springs, six grays, and four liveried outriders proclaimed his wealth.

Returning to M'sieur le Duc's enormous mansion on the Rue Saint-Honoré as his representative, it was as if the Duke himself had come home. No sooner had the carriage turned through the black and gold gates than word whipped through the labyrinth of servant passageways and the family's spacious rooms like an uncontrolled fire, scattering servants to the four corners of the buildings. And that fire burned most brightly in the apartment Lady Estée shared with her husband, and where she was to be found languishing on a chaise longue, a lady's maid at the ready with porcelain bowl and smelling salts. Yet word of the Duke's carriage had her sitting up and calling for her hand mirror. She had more than a few words to say to her brother. She might be ill, dying almost, but that did not mean she should not look her best for him.

The valet's instructions were clear: He was to fetch a red leather *portefeuille* presently locked in a drawer of the Duke's writing desk. The Duke told him where to find the hidden key. And he was not to return to the Versailles villa without the Duke's Parisian tailor and his two assistants, and with whatever instruments of their vocation and quantity of good dark cloth they required to carry out a fitting for a gentleman's ensemble. The other occupant of the carriage, who was to join them on the return journey, and the one which surprised the valet most, was his immediate subordinate and understudy, George Geraghty.

There simply was not room enough at the villa for all the Duke's personal attendants, so the under-valet had been left behind, in charge of making an inventory of the Duke's Parisian wardrobe and to see to the laundering, maintenance, repair, and renewal of any articles of clothing found to be wanting. Yet, not a fortnight later, the Duke now required the under-valet's services at the villa? This was greatly unsettling to Martin Ellicott. Not only had he not been consulted, Geraghty's presence was unnecessary. So why had he been summoned?

This question punctuated his thoughts throughout the day and returned to the forefront of his mind when he was kept waiting half an hour to be admitted into the presence of the Lady Estée Vallentine. It gave him time to ruminate on the whys and wherefores of the Duke requiring the particular presence of George Geraghty. Still without a satisfactory answer, he stepped into Madame's perfumed boudoir and was assailed by the twin forces of a strong, sweet-smelling scent and a caustic castigation, which numbed his senses. He heard only one word in ten, but kept his features in a state of effortless neutrality. When he was finally permitted to take his leave, a bundle of letters was thrust at his chest, as the Duke predicted, with strict instructions for their distribution, which he instantly ignored. A thudding headache that stayed with him for the rest of the day he attributed to the Lady Estée's overpowering flowery scent. It was no small wonder to him why the Duke's sister was suffering from nausea; he did not think her pregnancy entirely to blame.

FOUR

THE DUKE was being helped into a pair of over-the-knee black leather riding boots with enormous cuffs, when Antonia appeared in the doorway.

She was dressed *en déshabillé.* Over her lace-edged chemise were a pair of quilted jumps, loosely laced across her breasts with silk ribbons, and under a silk banyan that had slid off one shoulder, a matching quilted petticoat kept her stockinged legs warm. Her hair was in one long messy plait, the ends tied off with a ribbon, as if braided in a hurry and then forgotten. There was a tinge of color to her cheeks, because she had rushed the length of the apartment, thinking the Duke might have already departed to join the hunt. But seeing him, and that he was still being dressed, she stopped herself from going further into the room and allowed her heart to quiet.

There was a time when she would have swept up to him without a thought to who was there or what was going on, to tell him whatever was on her mind. That was before her sister-in-law's incessant lecturing on Antonia's twin responsibilities of being a duchess and a mother.

Estée was constantly reminding her that now she was a duchess, and not just any duchess, but *his duchess*, Antonia had to be mindful of her position at all times. That whatever she did, whatever she said, and however she conducted herself, she would always be watched and reported on to others, particularly those who wished to harm the Duke. Did she want to sabotage in one year what her husband had spent two decades avoiding? And Estée was not referring to his rakish past but the type of scandal all noble families wished to avoid, or suffer social ridicule.

The family, more particularly Roxton, had narrowly escaped being at the center of one of the biggest scandals of the age, when the Duke had eloped with Antonia under the nose of his cousin the Comte de Salvan. Never mind the Comte had schemed to marry Antonia to his mad son and then take her as his mistress. What mattered to Society were the formalities, and the fact there had been a binding marriage contract between Antonia's grandfather and the Comte. That was more important than the Comte's questionable morals, his son's insanity, and Antonia's innocence.

In eloping with Antonia, the Duke had acted like a common brigand and a societal *provocateur*. But in the eyes of many, particularly the ladies of the Court, it was Antonia's behavior which was far worse and unforgiveable. Despite being formally betrothed to the Comte de Salvan's heir, she had allowed herself to be seduced by a notorious rake. By deliberately putting herself in his orbit she had bewitched the Duke into acting dishonorably, and counter to his noble principles. Was it any wonder he had seduced her?

It required the personal intervention of Louis, with a public display of support for his good friend Roxton, to quell the private outrage of the courtiers calling for the Duke to be banished with a *lettre de cachet*. It would require further intervention by His Majesty if Antonia were ever to be accepted as Mme la Duchesse d'Roxton. The rehabilitation of her good character would begin with her official presentation at Court. And woe betide she took a misstep, for the vultures were circling, waiting to socially devour her, and in turn, M'sieur le Duc d'Roxton.

And here they were now, in this villa on the edge of the royal parkland, preparing for her official Court reception to Their Majesties. There were exacting steps required of her to be presented. She must be fitted for a ludicrously expensive court gown, have instruction in strict Court etiquette and in the language of the Court, for French nobles spoke with an inflection that was peculiar to them alone. And she must be presented by a female sponsor of impeccable virtue and nobility. Once she had made her curtsey to the Queen and then separately to the King, with the entire Court watching on, the Roxtons would be welcomed into the fold once again. Most importantly for the Duke, having made her public curtsey, Antonia could then accompany him to His Majesty's many little private suppers held in the *appartement* of his official mistress, Madame de Pompadour.

All this Antonia was prepared to do and more, knowing how important this piece of aristocratic theater was to the Duke's social well-being. And now that they had a son, and the Duke an heir, she had his future to think of as well, which made it imperative she be the best duchess she could be for them. All of this raced through her mind while she waited in the doorway, so wrapped in thought that the Duke had to repeat his question.

ROXTON NOTICED her want of dress and the pair of jumps in particular and guessed why she was still in the dressing stage. He waved aside his attendants, and held out his hand to her.

"You fed him this morning, *ma fée?*"

"I did. In my bath," she told him matter-of-factly. When he blinked, she added with a quizzical frown, "That shocks you?"

"No. It surprises me."

"Gabrielle and my women, they were shocked. But I do not

think Céleste she was," Antonia mused. "So perhaps she too has fed an infant while in a bath. But I think it more likely that as a wet nurse she placidly accepts it is the hungry infant who must be accommodated above all other considerations." She threw up a hand. "I ask you, Monseigneur, what else was I to do? Julian he does not care that his maman is in her bath up to her breasts in soap bubbles! All he cares about is having access to those breasts, and immediately."

The Duke suppressed a grin and enquired casually, "You did not think, as you were—er—indisposed, his immediate needs would have been best catered to by either nurse, so you could enjoy your bath?"

Antonia looked at him askance. "I did think it. But to do so would have been selfish. Julian had *two* feeds in the night, and Céleste and Cécile must also provide for their own babies, too. That is the understanding we made with them, yes? Besides," she added on a pout. "I must still do this for a little while longer yet."

"What? Feed our son in your bath?"

"Silly!" Antonia chuckled and felt better for it. She pressed herself against him and tilted her chin up for a kiss. "Thank you."

He enveloped her in his arms. "For what, *ma belle*?"

"For making me *un peu moins découragée*. Sometimes—and I know this will not shock you in the least—babies are fatiguing in the extreme."

"Yes. They are. And far more so for you. But we are making progress, yes? Our son is thriving. And why would he not, with two experienced wet nurses at his beck and call day and night? And they give his maman respite from his demands. All that matters is that he is healthy, and you are free of worry. Everything else will work itself out in time."

"If by working itself out, you are referring to weaning Julian off my breast, I know I must be patient. But I am not, Renard. I am very impatient. I am finding it as onerous to wean him as it was to have him first suckle." Antonia frowned. "My son he has a bad mother."

"You are too harsh on yourself, *ma vie*. Our son has been at your breast, day and night, for three months. As I told you, the vast majority of the ladies at Court never see their infants after they are born, least of all suckle them. They are sent away to the surrounding villages to be nursed."

"I could never do such a thing! I want our son with us, always. It is just that I cannot suckle him anymore because—because—"

"And why should you?" he interrupted. And to divert her from further self-castigation and a dilemma that had already been settled with the hiring of Morvan wet nurses, he added with an air of flippancy, "If I may offer a suggestion which will help you be more comfortable during this weaning stage…" And having her full attention he said with forced solemnity, "I am told that the application of cold cabbage leaves to each breast works wonders in reducing discomfort and—er—unnecessary swelling."

Antonia stared up at him, lips parted. "Cabbage leaves?"

"*Cold* cabbage leaves, *ma petite*."

"How do you know this about cold cabbage leaves? I believe it. But how do you know?"

"It was told to me by—"

Antonia kissed him swiftly, stopping his words. "No! Do not tell me! I know the females in your past life, they were many and varied, but—" A sparkle came into her green eyes. "Never would I have guessed you had bedded a woman with—with—" She giggled and moved in his arms. "—with vegetable matter covering her breasts!"

He pretended to be affronted and held her a little tighter. "You were not listening. I said I was told."

Antonia brushed this off. "Yes. The woman in the cabbage leaves she told you. Bed, blanket, or chaise, where this encounter took place it is unimportant. But these cabbage leaves they interest me vastly."

"Then may I suggest you send to the kitchen and have several sent up in a pail of ice. When I return, I will be interested to know if they do indeed provide you with relief."

He released her as a liveried attendant appeared in the doorway. The servant brought the news that the Duke's grooms, dogs, and horses were awaiting him at his earliest convenience.

"I had hoped to see you off in the courtyard, but I am not dressed. So I will do so from the gallery windows," Antonia told him as he collected his snuffbox and a pair of black leather riding gloves from the dressing table.

"Did you come here thinking I had departed without saying goodbye?" he asked with that uncanny ability to read her feelings and thoughts. When she nodded, he touched his forehead to hers and looked into her eyes with a smile. "I will never leave without a kiss from my wife. I will always find you to say *au revoir*."

"Thank you. But if it is because your father he left for the hunt and you did not say goodbye—"

"—and he broke his neck while on that hunt? That may have something to do with it, yes. But the truth is I do not like to be away from you at any time, hunt or no."

"It is the same with me. But sometimes it cannot be helped, and that I accept." She caressed his clean-shaven cheek. "You will not break your neck. You are a fine horseman. Besides, I will not allow it. And," she added, green eyes shining with mischief. "You must come home to me. I cannot lie around covered in cabbage leaves forever."

He gave a shout of laughter, then kissed her again. "I shall hold to that delightful picture in my mind's eye. It will see me return to you all the sooner." He had a sudden thought and became serious. "Antonia, you do know that regardless of my—er—*history*, no other woman compares to you—none. I find you—I find you— *endlessly fascinating*."

"Ah! Monseigneur, you did not need to say it," she replied with a tremulous smile, eyes damp. "But I will always love to hear you tell me. *Au revoir, mon amour.*"

"*Au revoir, ma vie.*"

And he was gone with a swish of his velvet skirts, the liveried attendant with the Duke's hat, sword, and silver hip flask quick to fall in behind his master as he strode off down the *enfilade.*

No sooner had the Duke left their apartment than Antonia rushed through the villa to the gallery.

Here it seemed the entire household were congregated. Men and women with children clutching to skirts or held up on a hip, were crowded against the row of windows that went the length of the long room. Some had their noses pressed to the glass, and all were transfixed by the activity in the stable courtyard below. Everyone was silent. No one noticed that Mme la Duchesse d'Roxton was behind them. Then one of the nursery maids turned to check on the occupant in the cradle she was rocking, saw her mistress, and so far forgot herself that she blurted out,

"Mme la Duchesse! *Sa Majesté! Sa Majesté!* He is here!"

FIVE

Antonia did not go straight to the windows, but to the cradle the nursery maid was rocking to and fro. She smiled down at her son and tickled his belly. When he let out an involuntary squeal of delight and kicked out his bare chubby legs and arms in greeting, she carefully scooped him up, white blanket and all, and kissed his rosy cheek.

"Shall we wave to your handsome papa on his horse?" she asked sweetly, and turned to the windows.

But she found herself blocked by a wall of backs, three deep. She was not pleased her servants were distracted, but if in truth the King was below, she understood their excitement and preoccupation. It was not every day, or any day, ordinary subjects saw their king or his courtiers at such close quarters. The chateau might be open to the public to stroll the gardens and enter the public rooms, but the King was always surrounded by the nobles of his court, and protected by a contingent of Swiss Guards. And no one could approach him who had not first been introduced.

"Make way! Make way!" Lord Vallentine ordered, breaking Antonia from her distraction and stepping in front of her to shoulder through the throng. "Make way, I say! Just 'cause you lot ain't at the hotel, don't think you can do as you please! Now scatter! Mme la Duchesse needs the view!"

Footmen quickly came to their senses, bowed, and returned to their posts. Nursery maids scooped up clinging infants and scuttled away. Antonia's own ladies, and her personal maid Gabrielle, who were amongst the onlookers, quickly dropped to a deep curtsey under Lord Vallentine's disapproving eye. With a guilty blush and gaze lowered to the parquetry, they shuffled backwards out of the way, allowing their young mistress to carry her son to the windows.

"This is what Estée was talkin' about," Vallentine complained, as he stepped aside so Antonia could be at the window. "Keep visitin' below stairs, and this lot will continue to take liberties. Got to keep a proper distance, now you're a duchess."

Antonia frowned up at him, with no idea as to what he was talking about.

"I do not understand. Liberties? Proper distance? Later you will please explain this to me. But now Julian he needs to wave to *son père*." She smiled at her son, adjusted her hold on him so his back was up against her chest and he facing the window, and peered down into the courtyard, saying in the voice she used with him, "Do you see *ton père, mon cher fils*? Do you?"

"The way they're carryin' on, you'd think they'd never seen a party set off for a hunt," Lord Vallentine continued with a huff. "That, or the King of France has come callin'!"

This last sentence he said with a laugh and shake of his head in disbelief. But it made Antonia stare up at him nonplussed.

"But... Vallentine, it *is* the King of France down there in the courtyard with Monseigneur."

"Eh? What?"

Antonia turned back to the view. "Open your eyes. Do you not see him? He is the one wearing violet in a sea of black."

"Violet?" Vallentine pulled a face. "God-awful color on a female. Worse on a man."

Antonia giggled. "His Majesty does not wear violet because he chooses to, but because it is tradition for the King to do so during mourning. And as His Majesty is still mourning the tragic loss of the Dauphine, he wears it for her. And the color it is unimportant because he is very handsome in whatever color he wears. More handsome than on the coins."

"Don't let Roxton hear you say so," Vallentine said darkly.

"You are being ridiculous. I am stating fact. And Monseigneur he would agree with me. Juju! Look! There is *ton père*," she breathed softly near her son's ear, adding in admiration, "M'sieur le Duc has the best seat of all the riders. One day you will too, *mon biquet*."

"He always looks damn fine astride a horse, don't he," Vallentine agreed. "And even with everyone else wearing black like him, Roxton still manages to outshine 'em all."

"But of course," Antonia agreed, a sly glance up at him. "He is the best at everything—"

"—except with a sword," Vallentine cut in, rising to her bait. "He's not as good as me with a rapier."

"No. But Monseigneur he is better at everything else," Antonia stated. "That you cannot dispute. And he is more handsome. That too is fact."

"Now look, how a person appeals to another person is a matter of opinion," Vallentine started to argue and was cut off.

"Juju! Look! *Ton père* he sees us!" Antonia exclaimed, catching up her infant's chubby fingers and waving his hand at the window.

Her excitement was infectious and her infant squealed his delight, kicking out his little bare legs and flapping his arms. Antonia laughed at his antics but held him a little more tightly to make certain she had a secure hold on him, for all his wriggling.

Vallentine rolled his eyes and clapped a hand to his forehead, wondering what those below in the courtyard, particularly the

Duke, would make of such a spectacle. He could only hope that with all the commotion they might have been distracted.

But what had been ordered chaos just minutes before, was now eerily quiet, the courtyard deserted of stable boys, ostlers, and farriers, now their work was done. A handful of liveried outriders of the King's own Swiss Guard had moved off too, back out under the archway, along the path beside the walled garden into the parkland beyond. Here the rest of the hunt party was congregating. Coming up over the hill cantered a company of noblemen, liveried outriders with hunting horns, and others with flintlock rifles. Behind them came the runners and followers with beating sticks, and the packs of dogs, while at the rear was another contingent of mounted Swiss Guard.

Only the Duke remained astride his mount in the center of the courtyard, and with him was the King of France in all his violet glory. They had brought their mounts to a standstill, facing the villa, backs to the commotion over the wall, and were in easy conversation. The King was smiling at something the Duke said. And then Roxton turned his head, looked up at the bank of windows of the gallery, and straight at Antonia. It was as if he knew she was there all along, and was just waiting for the ideal moment to break conversation to let her know that he did.

Their eyes locked.

Antonia's heart gave the oddest little flutter and she felt a flush of heat to her face. And when her duke smiled at her with his dark eyes, mouth barely turning up, in that way that was for her alone, she smiled back with a sigh, unconsciously voicing her admiration.

"No one outshines M'sieur le Duc, not even the King of France."

"Them's treasonous words," Vallentine quipped, then leaned sideways to say under his breath, "You'd best make your curtsey like the rest of his subjects at your back. Even if he ain't Roxton's lord and master, he is king of this dominion…"

That broke the spell. Antonia sensed her ladies had dropped to the parquetry. And when Vallentine also paid his respects with a flourishing bow, her gaze darted from the Duke to the King.

And there was Louis, King of France, acknowledging her with a raise of his feather-trimmed violet tricorne.

Antonia instantly dropped to a low curtsey, as best she could, holding her squirming infant son to her bodice. And when she rose up, with Vallentine's help at her elbow, the King replaced his hat, turned his mount, and headed out of the courtyard. The Duke remained a moment longer, looking up at her. Antonia blew him a kiss with a smile. He winked at her in response. He then turned his mount and followed the King out into the parkland to join the rest of the hunt.

"Wait until Estée hears Louis tipped his hat to you!" Vallentine declared with chuckle. "And you makin' your curtsey with your infant. Ha! I'll wager that's a new one on Louis, too!"

"None of that is important now," Antonia said dismissively. She kissed her son's chubby cheek and held him out to his uncle. "Please take your nephew over to his nurses. I must finish dressing, and then I have a letter for you to read."

"Letter?" Vallentine asked, taking the infant without a second thought. Too late he realized he now held a baby in a short chemise who was naked from the waist down, the white blanket that had been wrapped about him having fallen to the floor. He was kicking his legs freely in the air with great delight and gurgling. "Hey! Hey! He's not wearing breeches!"

"Breeches? Babies they do not wear breeches until they become little boys. You were a boy. You must know these things."

"Why? Why should I know? I don't remember *not* wearing breeches," Vallentine called out plaintively as Antonia swept away, her ladies falling in behind her. "Hey! Damme! What am I—what am I supposed to do with him?"

SIX

L ord Vallentine waited for Antonia to dress by spending a pleasant hour wandering about the villa, strolling the many *enfilades* and stairwells, and poking his nose into spacious, well-appointed rooms. Some were sparsely furnished with gilded, silk-covered sofas and chairs, and deep carpets, while others were occupied by workmen of various trades, engaged in stripping back old paint, repainting, carving, and refitting each room with large mirrors, over mantels, furniture, and *objets d'art*. He even went so far as to look behind more than one of the concealed doors in the paneling. Here he often found himself confronted by a liveried footman or two, or a maid, busily employed in dusting, polishing, changing out candles, and generally engaged in the day-to-day running of a noble household.

He wasn't the most astute observer of the habits and opinions of servants but he sensed they were happier here at this villa than they were at the Parisian hotel. Not least, he was certain, because unlike the cavernous mansion owned by his best friend which was difficult to heat, this villa had warmth to every room.

Here there was a Dutch ceramic heater in the foyer and two in the long gallery, and he was told by a servant servicing the one in the foyer that there was a fourth in the private apartments occupied by the Duke and Duchess. A system of pipes connected these heaters, dispensing warmth throughout the villa.

But he also guessed servant contentment had to do with the fact they were out from under his wife's exacting eye. For almost a decade Estée had been mistress at the hotel, and so the household had come under her purview. But now Roxton was married and had a duchess, the running of the ducal household was no longer his wife's concern, it was Antonia's—and there was the rub. He knew Estée was finding it difficult to relinquish control; more concerning was her uncanny knack to find fault with the Duchess's every action and decision. And with two strong-willed women living under the same roof, albeit a very large roof, life at the hotel had become strained.

And having had time to think about it while he wandered the rooms of this villa, Vallentine concluded that there really was no wondering why Roxton had left Paris with his duchess and baby son and brought them here! Had he himself not fled the hotel and his wife? He had a twinge of guilt at leaving her while she was in the depths of misery due to morning sickness. But it was just a twinge, and it soon passed, because she had foolishly wished him anywhere but near her. And as he was needed here by the Duke, and more importantly by Antonia, he had fallen in with his wife's wishes, and no doubt far too quickly for her liking.

And he would have to take back his remark about the house being a dog box. He should have known Roxton would not live in anything but spacious splendor. Now having his bearings and been all over this residence, inside and out, he realized this villa had at one time been two separate townhouses. The gallery, which Antonia had turned into an expansive nursery for her son, his nurses, and their children, connected one townhouse to the other on the upper level, while at street level an orangery cloister ran between the two, either side of the *porte-cochère.*

The frontage that looked out on the avenue still gave the impression of two separate dwellings, sharing the *porte-cochère* with its set of enormous, blue-painted wooden double doors that kept out the world. The covered carriage entrance was wide enough for the largest travelling coach to stop inside a deep alcove that protected its occupants from the elements. Here passengers were set down and immediately passed into an expansive entrance foyer with black and white tiles and a polished-marble curved staircase. On the first landing, *enfilades* stretched left and right. And as Vallentine discovered from his self-guided tour, while guests could turn right, they could not go left. Left, they were met by two sentry-like footmen guarding the entrance to the Duke and Duchess's private apartments.

He had come full circle and was back in the warmth and light of the gallery, and was surprised to find Antonia waiting for him. She was over by the windows in the oblique sunlight, hair swept up and held in place with an assortment of pins and gold and bejeweled hair ornaments. Over her quilted petticoats and pair of jumps was an open robe gown of burgundy velvet, and she wore half boots and carried a large fur muff. One of her ladies was with her and had a fur-lined hooded jacket over her arm, ready for when her mistress stepped outside into the garden.

The gallery was not as rowdy as when he had left it after handing over the precious ducal infant to his nurses. Half a dozen small children were either being fed, entertained, or supervised at the far end, while at the other end, behind a few well-placed privacy screens, a couple of cradles were occupied by sleeping infants. They were being watched over by maids, seated in the light from the windows, engaged in needlework and low whispered conversation.

Vallentine sauntered across to Antonia with a smile and was about to compliment her when she turned, looked him up and down, and asked with an impish smile,

"Why do you have your sword? Are we under attack—from babies?"

"Droll!" He subconsciously rested a gloved hand on his sword hilt and stuck out his cleft chin. "It pays to remain vigilant. You can never be too careful."

Antonia frowned in puzzlement. "But if there were danger, M'sieur le Duc he would not have gone off to hunt with the King, yes? What is it you are not telling me?"

"Tellin' you? Eh?" He put up his gloved hands in capitulation. "But you were the one who sent for me, remember?"

"I did," Antonia replied with satisfaction. "I apologise. You are right. You can never be too careful. So I will gratefully accept your sword and your protection because Monseigneur he would be unhappy if I did not have it. You will see what I mean when you have read the letter." She threaded her arm through his. "Come. Let us go out into the garden while the sun is still out and," she added in a whisper near his ear, up on tiptoe, "where we will not be overheard."

Out of doors, and wearing her hooded jacket, gloved hands deep in a fur muff, Antonia stepped off the terrace and onto a garden path that led to a pond with an ornate fountain being repaired by a team of workmen. Lord Vallentine was beside her, a long coat over his frock, and hands deep in its pockets. Antonia's maid followed them, but as instructed, kept her distance so the couple could speak freely without feeling their every word was being overheard.

They had not strolled far when Antonia stopped on the path and produced a letter with a broken seal from deep within the muff. She held it up.

"I received this from *Grand-mère* a month ago," she told him. "It was when Madame was first struck down with the morning sickness. I know that if she had not been ill, she would have asked me about it, and I could not have lied to her. But I have not said a word to M'sieur le Duc all this time because—because he would not be pleased with *Grand-mère*."

"I don't know why I'm tellin' you this," Vallentine said in what he hoped was a solemn tone, "because you know it better than anyone, but you'll never keep anythin' from Roxton where his family is concerned. But most particularly if it involves *you*. I'll wager he already knows what's in that letter, and more!"

Antonia shrugged. "I know M'sieur le Duc has my best interests at heart. That does not concern me in the least. But this…?" She shook her head and stuck out her lip. "No. He does not know what is in this."

"How can you be sure?"

"Because the consequences of knowing, they have not happened. But if and when he does find out…" She gave a little shudder then turned and grabbed Vallentine's forearm. "You and I —*we*—will put a stop to it before those consequences they occur. But I see that you are still in the deep darkness, so I will explain it to you."

"If you wouldn't mind. But before you begin—and I shouldn't say this because the woman is your grandmother. So instead let me say it about her as the Lady Strathsay. That woman is a viper, a jealous, vengeful viper. She'll do anythin' to upset you, you know that, don't you?"

Antonia nodded. "Yes. That is all true. She is the only blot on our lives, except for this letter. So there are two blots which have become one big blot!"

"Tell me about this big blot and what that viper wrote, *ma petite sœur*," Vallentine said gently. "And I'll do whatever it takes to help you."

"*Merci, cher beau-frère.* I know M'sieur le Duc and I can always rely on you. And it is not what *Grand-mère* wrote, it is what she has done," Antonia answered cryptically.

The sag to her shoulders and accompanying soft sigh was enough to make Vallentine silently grind his teeth. And when she looked up at him with a brave smile and hope in her green eyes, he would have agreed to anything to take the burden of worry from her. What she said next made his mouth drop open.

"It is just that I do not want Monseigneur to kill anyone."

He gave a start. "*Kill?* Eh? Are you certain?"

Antonia nodded. "But of course. Do you think I do not know Monseigneur better than anyone?"

"That's not in dispute." Vallentine leaned into her and asked softly, "You want me to kill them instead?"

It was Antonia's turn to flinch.

"*Quoi?* No! No! No! No one is to die, Vallentine! You and I we must arrange for it all to go away before M'sieur le Duc he finds out."

Vallentine shook his head. "I'm all for doin' that, but let's be matter-of-fact. He's goin' to find out and he'll do what's necessary, and if it is a question of honor—"

"But of course it is a question of honor!" Antonia repeated, squaring her shoulders. "You think M'sieur le Duc would kill someone for less? And that is why he must not find out, and why I cannot tell him, and why you will help me."

"Perhaps you had best start at the beginnin' and tell me what this is all about," he suggested.

"We are here so I can do just that. And why we are out in the freezing air."

"I understand. You don't want Roxton's spies findin' out, and as a consequence, him discoverin' what you know that he don't."

"Yes, and no. True I do not want Monseigneur to know. But equally I do not want *Grand-mère* finding out how upsetting this is for me. And she will. She seems to know my every move without me telling her."

"There's a spy in Roxton's household?" Vallentine was aghast. "Jesus! You're not wrong about there bein' a killin'. Blood will be spilled when he discovers the traitor. Do you have any idea who it might be?"

Antonia frowned. "I do not understand. Why is it you are shocked that my grandmother has a spy in our household, when M'sieur le Duc he has spies everywhere?!"

"That's different. She's a viper. He's not."

"And that makes it acceptable? No! No! I do not want to argue the philosophical with you. There is no time. I would need to compile a list—"

"*List*?!" Vallentine hissed, hand to his sword hilt and a look over his shoulder as if expecting imminent danger. "How many spies are we talkin' about?" And then he had a sudden thought. Frowning down at Antonia, he asked with evident disappointment, "These spies, they aren't women, are they?"

"What has that got to do with anything? A spy is a spy."

"I can't stick a sword in a woman."

"That is as well because of course it must be a woman if she is—"

"Shame. Damme."

"—spying on me to *Grand-mère*. But she—that spy—she is not our immediate concern. You can leave that spy to me. I only tell you about her because it is part of the bigger blot… And now by your cod face I can tell you have no idea what I am talking about!" Antonia giggled and grabbed Vallentine's sleeve. "Come! I think it best if I stop talking now and show you, and then you will understand."

"I think that wise," Vallentine muttered and let Antonia go before him down the path that led to the pond.

The pond had been drained for winter repairs and refurbishment, and half a dozen workmen were dismantling a fountain that formed the centerpiece of this garden feature. Antonia walked on, preoccupied with the letter she held. But they, to a man, stood straight and doffed their caps as she and Vallentine passed by, before resuming their work.

Antonia continued on to an arbor, and here she stopped and opened out the letter from her grandmother, Augusta, Countess of

Strathsay. The Countess's note was brief and was all about the letter she had enclosed within hers. Antonia did not mention what her grandmother had written, there was no need to. What only mattered was this second letter, and who had written it, and why.

Antonia gave it to her brother-in-law.

"This was wrapped inside *Grand-mère's* letter. It is addressed to me, but it was sent to her. You will understand why it was not sent directly, and why I am in a dilemma, and why I have not told M'sieur le Duc about its existence, when you see who it is from. Never mind what he writes."

Vallentine took the letter, gaze on Antonia, and it remained on her while he opened up the single page of parchment written on both sides. He only dropped his gaze to the ink when she took a step away and looked back at the house.

He did not immediately start reading but turned the letter over and went straight to the signature at the lower left-hand side. It was done in a flourishing fist, and beside it was a red wax seal which had pressed into it the coat of arms of an ancient noble family of France.

Lord Vallentine's head jerked up, his light blue eyes closed to slits, and his mouth twisted up with revulsion. He could barely say the name, and when he did it came out in a hoarse whisper full of loathing.

"*Salvan.*"

SEVEN

When you leave England, I never want to see your face
again... If ever you approach the Duchess for any reason, I
will kill you. If you ever cause her the slightest distress, be this
the mere mention of your name in connection with my family,
or you cause a rumor of any description to reach my wife's ears,
I will kill you...

THESE CHILLING WORDS, spoken by the Duke to his cousin the Comte de Salvan a mere ten months ago, were etched in Vallentine's brain for all time. So too the image of Roxton delivering this threat before turning his back on Salvan forever. The Comte's terror at the realization the Duke meant every word was small compensation. Vallentine had demanded nothing less than the Comte's death for his appalling part in the horrific attack on the Duchess and her unborn son. And yet, despite coming close to losing her life, and miscarrying her child, Antonia had not wanted her perpetrators—Salvan and his mad son—killed. The Duke had acquiesced.

But Vallentine doubted his friend would be lenient a second time.

And now he had in his hand proof Salvan had flouted the Duke's warning! Had the man lost his mind entirely? Because all it would take was for the Duke to hear of this letter's existence, never mind having it thrust under his nose, and he would go post-haste to Limoges and make good on his threat. By Vallentine's reckoning, Salvan had mere weeks to live.

It boiled his blood that the Frenchman had dared to write to Antonia, but to think it was her grandmother who was the conduit by which the Comte had gained access to the Duchess, infuriated him.

"I take back what I said about not sticking a sword into a female," he spat out, letter crumpling as his fingers convulsed in anger. "I'll make an exception of that-that—*she-devil* you have for a grandmother!"

"Vallentine! Do not crush it before you have read it!"

His Lordship pulled a face. "Must I? I know who it's from. I can see it's upset you greatly. That's more than enough and all I need to—"

"No. It is not enough. Please," Antonia asked quietly. "Please read it and then you will know why I have not told Monseigneur."

Hearing her distress cooled his anger considerably and he said no more, nodded and dropped his gaze to the letter. But he did not read at once. He needed to take a few deep breaths before he could steel himself to discover what the disgraced and reviled nobleman had ventured to write to the Duchess of Roxton.

And Salvan was taking an almighty risk. For after the Duke's threat to kill him, Vallentine expected Salvan to do the decent thing and put an end to his own life. King Louis had banished him from the French Court to his estate in the south of France. And there he was to remain for the rest of his natural life. Vallentine pictured the nobleman cowering away in the shadows of his crumbling chateau, one eye always looking over his shoulder, in anticipation of being murdered, either by one of the King's musketeers, or by an assassin in Roxton's pay. The last thing Vallentine expected was for the fiend to write to the one person on this earth that would surely bring a swift ignoble end to his life.

"Read it," Antonia insisted, finger flicking the parchment to break Vallentine out of his abstraction. "I will walk while you do."

He watched her stroll off down the path between a grove of shaped linden trees aflame with bright autumnal yellow leaves, her lady's maid a few steps behind. And when she stooped to pick up a leaf, it brought him out of his thoughts. He dropped his gaze to the tightly sloping script of the Comte de Salvan, first cousin of his best friend the Duke of Roxton, and of his wife Estée.

Madame la Duchesse

I write not to offend you, or to cause you the slightest distress, but to humbly request your favor.

It is a grand presumption, and I have no right to do so. The mere fact you have received a letter by my hand has no doubt caused you pain. I can only hope that your grandmother in her infinite wisdom prepared you for this letter from me. And so, I humbly request your forgiveness and understanding, and I pray that you will grant me this because you possess the sweetest of temperaments.

But enough of my compliments which you no doubt think insincere and trite, and which must offend you, coming as they do from someone whom you judge to be the most evil creature put on God's earth.

You can believe me or not when I say that poor Salvan has spent every waking hour of every day of his banishment in regret for his odious actions towards you. I do not say so to gain your forgiveness or to receive clemency from your noble husband. I know mon cousin will never entertain the notion that I could be repentant, and that he will never offer me a scintilla of mercy. That is as it should be. And if you decide to show him this letter, or to mention I have communicated with you, I am confident of a visit from him or one of his agents, and my time on earth will end at the point of a sword very soon in the future.

So why does poor Salvan write to you at the risk of losing what is left of his most miserable life?

Because I wish to save another from the fate I have suffered at the hands of your noble husband.

You must know as the world knows it—the fate and future of my family rests solely in the hands of M'sieur le Duc d'Roxton. Whether my name lives on after me. Whether we Salvans prosper or fall. Whether we are ever to return to Court, or are able to marry well ever again. All of it is at the whim of mon cousin. It is to him His Majesty listens, and it is to him all others look to see how they themselves are to comport with any member of the Salvan family.

That I am reviled is fit punishment for my sins. But poor Salvan asks you, no he <u>begs</u> you to consider if the rest of his family, who had no part in his ridiculous schemes—not even his sad son who was not in his right mind—should suffer the inglorious fate of poor Salvan, all because of their blood connection. The Salvan name is now synonymous with treachery of the most base kind, for which I am solely to blame.

I do not believe for one moment that you want poor Salvan's family to suffer, to be social outcasts in perpetuity. I make this grand presumption because I have always known that there is no evil in you. And how do I know this? Because there is bad blood—evil—in me and my pathetic offspring. Dark can see light, even when the light is incapable of understanding the dark.

You have an untainted soul and a loving heart, and you have bestowed upon mon cousin M'sieur le Duc d'Roxton the gift of salvation. My hope against hope is that you will find it in your heart to also be my family's salvation—

VALLENTINE BROKE OFF and glanced up from the page, mouth tinder-dry, as if he had eaten a spoonful of ashes. Such was his revulsion for the Comte and his incredulity at the sincerity in his words that were it not for Antonia's wish he read the entire letter, he'd screw it up into a tight ball and fling it over the high garden wall. He did no such thing, and with an impatient grunt turned the parchment over to read the second page of tightly written script. Before he continued, he searched out Antonia, and found her stopped halfway down the linden grove.

A couple of workmen were raking leaves and adding them to a pile of burning detritus, the gently smoldering plumes of white-gray smoke curling up into a cloudless sky. Antonia was in conversation with one of these workmen, who had doffed his cap and was gesticulating and pointing to something beyond Vallentine's line of sight. No doubt the man was explaining something to her. She was ever inquisitive and enthusiastic about everything. It made His Lordship smile indulgently, but the smile dropped, and the taste of ash on his tongue returned when he read on, re-reading the last sentence of the first page before continuing.

—My hope against hope is that you will find it in your heart to also be my family's salvation.

For as surely as the sun rises every morning, there is no one on this earth who can appeal to M'sieur le Duc d'Roxton's better nature than you. He who cannot be swayed by others can be swayed by you. He who has never loved another, loves you beyond reason. You have the power, if you have the will, to persuade him to show my family clemency. Only you can save the Salvans from centuries of ignominy and ruin.

How do you do this? By opening your heart and your home to an innocent young man who is at the beginning of his life's journey. One small kindness from you is all I ask, no, I beg. To persuade M'sieur le Duc to deign to acknowledge the young man's existence in the smallest of ways—a nod, a word, a look of approval in company—and society would surely then embrace him, secure in the knowledge that while poor Salvan is shunned by M'sieur le Duc d'Roxton for all eternity, this young man who is also a Salvan, is not.

And so poor Salvan commends to you his late uncle's grandson, Hubert Gabriel Louis Hyacinth Salvan Montbelliard, the Chevalier Montbelliard.

The boy has the great misfortune of being my heir since the demise of my own poor son (may his tortured soul now rest in peace), and will inherit all my worldly goods, as well as the ancient family title and lands, when my miserable carcass finally breathes its last. He is also destined to inherit my shame and misfortune.

If he is not done the small kindness of being publicly acknowledge by mon cousin, then he Montbelliard will be forced to spend his life in exile, away from good society, away from all employment in the service of L'Majesty, and rejected as a suitable husband by all good families. This is the fate that awaits him when he becomes the Comte de Salvan, if you do not intervene on his behalf with mon cousin.

He is a good boy, a fine dutiful son to his widowed mother, and a protective brother to his four sisters. He is of excellent character and temperament. He has the highest integrity and is, in truth, unlike any Salvan that has come before him, which is his great good fortune. He will rehabilitate the name Salvan if given the opportunity. But do not take my word for it. I ask, no I plead with you, to decide your own mind by allowing him an audience so that you may judge him for yourself.

His fate and his future, and the future of the Salvan name, it is all in your hands, Mme la Duchesse d'Roxton.

Poor Salvan supplicates himself at your feet, body sprawled face down in the muck, willing to do anything and all that is necessary for you to do this one kindness, not for him, but for the Chevalier Montbelliard.

I would sign myself your most obedient servant but I know those words where I am concerned are meaningless to you. Instead I thank you for your time, your compassion, and your great goodness in accepting and reading this letter from poor Salvan.

Jean-Honoré Gabriel Salvan
Comte de Salvan
Château D'Ambert
Limoges

EIGHT

WITH THE LETTER dangling between his fingers, Lord Vallentine joined Antonia in the linden grove. The workmen had returned to raking the fallen leaves and were adding them to the smouldering pile.

"You read it all?" she asked as she gave her fur muff to her lady-in-waiting.

"I did; both ghastly pages. He never was one to get to the point, was he? No idea what you're goin' to do with it, though," he apologized, returning the letter. "Or how you're to keep it from Roxton. If that's your intention. You won't, y'know. Keep it from him. Hey! What—what are you doin'?"

"I am putting it to the flame," she answered calmly, having tossed the folded parchment atop the burning leaves. "I have read it and now so have you. And we are the only ones—aside from *Grand-mère*, who I am very sure did not send it to me without first reading it—who need to read it. Monseigneur does not. It will only upset him—"

"Ha! Understatement! And not so much the flowery pathetic

prose, but the audacity of that vile toad in writin' to you, and upsettin' you."

"I am not upset. I was. But I am not now," she replied, gaze on the burning paper turning to ash. With it folding in on itself she gave a little sigh and turned to face Vallentine with a smile. "I think of the present and the future, not the past. What happened all those months ago with Etienne and Salvan was truly awful, and at the time it distressed and saddened me. But I have put it all behind me. What matters is that I am married to Monseigneur, and that we love each other with all our hearts, and that we have a son, whom we both love dearly. They are my future and they make me happy."

"That's a mature way of lookin' at life," Vallentine mused, surprised. "You have wisdom beyond your years. Makes me feel the juvenile! Sometimes I forget you're a chit—"

"Vallentine! No! Maturity it has nothing to do with age," Antonia stated imperiously. "And you forget yourself. I am not a chit. I am a wife and a mother, and I am Mme la Duchesse d'Roxton."

"Forgive me, Mme la Duchesse." He made her a low elegant bow, points of color to his lean cheeks. "Indeed you are. I did not mean to offend—"

"No! No! Do not bow to me. I am sorry," she quickly apologized, and grabbing his arm to steady herself went up on tiptoe to swiftly kiss his cheek. "There is nothing spiteful about you. It is me. I am doing my best, but I still have much to learn. And I know that Madame, while she is reconciled to the fact I am now in charge of M'sieur le Duc's household, she thinks me incapable of running it to her satisfaction, and how she thinks it should be run for one so important as her brother."

"Estée is just jealous," Vallentine admitted truthfully. "Until you swept into Roxton's life she was the only female with whom he had ever shared a house. And," he added with a sheepish grin of guilt, "Roxton's lackeys serve Estée because she's his sister. But you

—aah! They serve you because they want to, and regardless their master is M'sieur le Duc d'Roxton. They'd do anythin' for you, y'know that, don't you?"

Antonia returned his guilty smile and blushed. "What you say, is what I thought, but hearing you say it makes me feel better. Thank you."

Vallentine lightly touched the tip of her little nose with the end of a gloved finger, and then touched the tip of his. "Between us."

She nodded with a smile. "Between us."

A large crack from the burning pile of garden refuse momentarily diverted them. It was a pinecone combusting, so one of the gardeners assured them. The diversion returned Antonia to the matter at hand. She took back her muff from her maid, and linking arms with her brother-in-law, they wandered away from the fire, strolling the path that led to an ornate gate in the high garden wall that opened out into the royal parkland beyond.

"Vallentine, I need to tell you that I do not think Monseigneur has put behind him that terrible incident," she confessed with a frown. "He told me once… There was a moment—when Etienne was hovering over me with the knife and my gown was covered in blood—when he thought he had lost me and our baby. He could not breathe. He was gripped with a tightness in his chest, a pain he says he experienced that must be what it is like when the heart it no longer beats." She glanced up at Vallentine, who was looking straight ahead, mouth in a grim line. "I think that truly frightened him, to come so close to losing us that his heart it stopped beating long enough to cause him pain. And he is not frightened of anything or anyone, is he?!"

"No. He is not."

"But with me and Julian…" She glanced up at him again, and he was still staring straight ahead, mouth now pulled down. "We —we are his weakness of the heart, yes? And he never thought he would ever have such a weakness, did he?"

"No. He did not."

"And the death of Gray… The hideous way in which Etienne he-he—"

"You do not need to say it. I remember," Vallentine said softly. "Roxton was—*is*—devoted to his dogs. Always has been. What happened to Gray is not somethin' anyone is likely to forget."

Antonia tugged on his arm to make him look down at her, and she stared up into his blue eyes.

"Vallentine, you must not repeat any of this to him, or to anyone. Not even to Madame. I do not keep secrets from him, but this… He does not need to know that we have talked about this. Promise me."

He nodded and said with none of his usual nonchalance, "On my honor." He hunched his shoulders against the cold. "If you want my opinion—"

"I do."

"He'll never forgive Salvan," he stated flatly. "Nor will he agree to that monster's pathetic, and quite frankly ludicrous, scheme for havin' this Hubert what's-his-name acknowledged by good society. You can try all you like to champion the lad's cause, if that is how you wish to proceed—and knowin' you and your capacity for forgiveness I'm pretty confident that's what you want to do. And you'll get Roxton to melt before you as only you can, but—but be damned if he'll budge an inch, even for you, the light of his life. Roxton will never give Salvan the satisfaction of knowin' the future of his bloodline is secure with Chevalier what's-his-name, if indeed he is who Salvan claims he—"

"But, Vallentine, Salvan he is not lying about Hubert Mont-belliard. He is his heir."

"And that mad son of his locked away in the Bicêtre? Aren't we all forgettin' d'Ambert?"

Antonia stopped and turned to face Vallentine, back to the high garden wall. She put up her chin with a little twisted knowing smile.

"Etienne is dead, Vallentine. You know it. Madame knows it. And so does M'sieur le Duc. The only person who you all think does not know is me! But I have known since just after it happened and M'sieur le Duc was informed of it. Poor Etienne he died on the return journey to France, drowning on the Channel crossing."

Vallentine did not try to deny it. "How did you find out—No! Let me guess. Old Grandmother Viper told you."

"She did. And that he was not thrown overboard on Salvan's wishes. The musketeers who were there to guard against that eventuality on the orders of Monseigneur confirmed this. *Grand-mère* she told me, and it was Salvan who told her, that Etienne he had a moment of lucidity while on the crossing to France. That he suddenly woke up to the true sordid nature of his life. The horror of killing Monseigneur's most devoted four-legged companion, and his attempt to kill me, it was all too much for him. He jumped ship and because he could not swim, he drowned."

"You feel sorry for him, even after all that he tried to do—"

"That monster was not Etienne. Of course I feel for the boy I knew. I am not happy he drowned, but I am glad he is now at peace. Something that was to be denied him had he been kept alive chained up in an asylum."

Vallentine pulled in his chin. "You do realise of course that it was on Roxton's orders he was to be kept in chains at Bicêtre?"

Antonia looked offended. "You think I disagree with M'sieur le Duc? Not at all! Renard was intent on locking away a monster to keep me and our baby safe. The boy who drowned was not that monster. But it does mean with Etienne's death, the monster is also dead. *Enfin.*"

"Aye. It does. And while the son may now rest in peace with his monster at the bottom of the sea, it don't mean Salvan should be given any sort of reprieve. Salvan made his son evil by feedin' him opiates. But Salvan wasn't made evil, he's just evil. And if you ask me, he's lucky to still be alive! Banishment was too good for him. I'm with Estée on this. Roxton should have stuck him there and then, and ended his miserable existence!"

Antonia was surprised. "But at the time you said death was too good for him. Banishment to his estate was better because he would have to live with what he did every day for the rest of his life. And yet now you think Monseigneur should've killed him on the spot?"

"I do."

Antonia thought about this a moment, and then shook her head.

"No. I cannot agree with you or Madame. If Salvan had died at the point of M'sieur le Duc's sword in our apartment at Treat, it would have remained a stain on our lives there. Did you not think of that? Of course you did not, but I am very sure Monseigneur he did."

Vallentine took a deep breath and nodded. "Aye, I see your point."

"You think when our friends and relatives they come to visit they want to be reminded that their host killed his cousin, a cousin who orchestrated an attack on me? You think we want to live with that memory? No! It is sad enough that we must live with the death of Gray in that horrible way. But we still have Tan, and when he and his new companion are reunited with their master, some of Monseigneur's sadness will disappear. No, Vallentine. Treat is to be a happy place, a place for us to bring up our children, where our friends and family will come to stay and enjoy themselves. That is to be the Treat of the fifth duke and his duchess. I am determined it will be so."

When Lord Vallentine stared at her, incredulous, a gloved hand to his mouth, Antonia frowned, thinking he meant to offer a counter-argument of some sort. And she was ready to argue the point with him.

But what Vallentine was thinking was something else entirely. He was remembering what his best friend had said to him the night before about what they had got up to as nineteen-year-olds and their inexperience of life when compared to the position and responsibility that now weighed on the shoulders of this delightful beauty before him. He couldn't imagine him or Roxton at the same age being as forward thinking, and family were a thousand fathoms beyond their consideration.

As for Treat—the ducal seat—the very idea of transforming such a cold marble edifice of monumental proportion, built specifically for the glorification and ever-lasting memorialization of the Roxton dukedom—into something which resembled a happy home, was so appealing in its simplicity that it caused Vallentine to let out a whoop of joy. And unable to contain himself, he threw up his arms and pirouetted on the spot.

"Huzza for happy days in your happy home, Mme la Duchesse!" he declared, and grabbing Antonia by the elbows, because her hands were dug deep in her muff, he danced about with her. "Finally Treat will live up to its name and be a treat, all thanks to you!"

Startled, she was slow to respond, but Vallentine's happiness was infectious and soon she was laughing and giggling and dancing around with him.

Antonia's maid stepped forward more than once, alarmed by such bizarre behavior, wondering if she should intervene and snatch her mistress away from the clutches of the eccentric Lord Vallentine. But in the end dizziness prevailed and the couple staggered to the nearest stone bench and once Vallentine had Antonia seated, he collapsed beside her.

After taking a moment to catch his breath, His Lordship said with a note of apology, "Forgive m' over-exuberance, but it makes me beyond delighted to hear you are goin' to turn that grim palace of despair into a place of joy for Roxton and you, and the rest of us."

"Grim palace of despair?" Antonia repeated, then smiled crookedly. "You dare to call Monseigneur's hotel a heap of old bricks and now you call his English country house a grim palace? It is a wonder you can bear to visit us for months on end in such a gloomy place!"

"It ain't gloomy now you're sharin' it with him," Vallentine stated. "You've cleared out all those old ghouls hauntin' the corridors. And there's none more ghoulish than Roxton's grandfather. Dreadful martinet! It's no wonder his own son up and left and never returned to English shores. As for what the fourth Duke did when he got his hands on Roxton as a boy. Egad! Sends shivers down m' spine thinkin' about it—"

Antonia sat up very tall. "*Quoi? Qu'est-ce qu'il a fait?*"

Vallentine shook his head and wagged his finger. "No. Not my place to say. I don't know it all, but what I do, and what I was witness to the one and only time I visited, is not for me to repeat. You'll have to ask Roxton y' self. Damme! And here was I hopin' to divert you with happy thoughts and deeds, and all I've done is sent your mind spinnin' in all directions. And you won't rest until you've found it all out. And Roxton won't thank me for it, will he?"

"Do not worry yourself," Antonia assured him, thrusting her muff back at her dazed maid. "I will ask him in a way that does not implicate you. I am always asking him questions, and he is very patient with me, and so I will find the appropriate moment to slip in the question about his grim grandfather."

Vallentine rolled his eyes. "Aye. I don't doubt you will. But he'll know it was me who told you." He shrugged. "So be it." He took out his pocket watch to note the time. "I was thinkin' about strollin' across to *La Grande Écurie* and showin' m' face at the fencin' school. So I hate to return to that letter you just put to the flame, but you've yet to give me a clear indication what it is you need from me. But if it's help with gettin' Roxton's public blessin' for Salvan's heir, the Chevalier what's-his-name, I'm afraid you've next to no hope of—"

"Vallentine! I do not understand why it is so difficult for you to remember the Chevalier's surname. Particularly when you know him very well indeed."

Vallentine was so astounded he was up off the bench and facing her, pocket watch left dangling on its silver chain from his velvet waistcoat pocket. "What? *Know him*? How do I know him?"

Antonia's green eyes widened and a secretive smile hovered about her lovely mouth.

"I do not think I should tell you here," she replied with a teasing sweetness. "You will know as soon as you see him."

Vallentine looked about swiftly, as if he expected the Chevalier Montbelliard to be breathing down his neck. He was not. He looked back at Antonia, who was now also on her feet, and his eyes narrowed.

"What's goin' on?"

Untroubled by his suspicion, Antonia put her arm through his and turned him toward the villa. She again put out her hand for her muff. "You are right. Time it is running on, and your guest he will be here waiting."

"Aye? Now what have you gone and done, Mme la Duchesse," Vallentine complained lamely.

He did not expect an answer. He knew when he had been outwitted. He silently strolled back to the villa, Antonia on his arm, who was fairly skipping beside him.

NINE

Antonia had barely put a half-boot onto the black and white tiles of the orangery cloister, when a liveried footman came scurrying down its length, weaving in and out amongst the large winter tubs of pear, apple, and lemon trees. He bowed and presented a silver salver that had upon it the visiting card of one Hubert Gabriel Louis Hyacinth Salvan Montbelliard, the Chevailer Montbelliard. The footman informed her that the Chevalier had been shown into the morning room. And as Mme la Duchesse had requested earlier, a silver coffee urn and an assortment of cakes were sent in upon the Chevalier's arrival.

And then to Vallentine's surprise, Antonia excused herself. He, Vallentine, would have to greet the Chevailer Montbelliard without her. She must visit her son and change out of her walking boots.

"But! But! Damme! What am I goin' to say to the fellow?" Lord Vallentine moaned, struggling to shrug out of his greatcoat as he followed her indoors.

A footman came to his aid and also took his gloves. But when Vallentine had second thoughts about unbuckling his sword, the footman stepped away. And then His Lordship just stood there in indecision. He was torn between doing as he was told and what Roxton would expect of him, and being accused of disloyalty, a traitor to friendship if he sat down to coffee and gateaux with the heir of Roxton's sworn enemy. And then the Duchess took him by surprise, fuelling his curiosity and embarrassment in equal measure so that he forgot about this dilemma entirely.

On the first landing, Antonia looked over the balustrade and down at Vallentine who remained in the foyer, vacillating.

"I know what you will say without me needing to be there to hear you say it. You will say what you always say. Later you will tell me if I am wrong." She disappeared from view before Vallentine could comment, but a moment later, and few steps up, she popped her head over again and called down, "Vallentine!? Do not touch the *Nougat de Montélimar*. Madame says it gives you wind. *À bientôt!*"

"For the love of all that's sacred," Vallentine muttered, wiping a hand over his flushed face and turning on a heel.

He looked up and caught the footman piled up with his coat and gloves, and one of his fellows over by the double doors, trying their best to stop themselves from bursting out laughing, which was only making their faces turn red and their shoulders shake. He took a step toward them, hand to his sword hilt, and growled. They instantly fell back, eyes wide and faces drained of color. Feeling better, His Lordship sauntered off.

It was only when a footman admitted him into the morning room that he remembered his initial dilemma of being torn between falling in with Antonia's plans and being disloyal to his best friend by acknowledging the Comte de Salvan's heir. But it was too late. He was in the room, and now he must go through with the introduction.

"M'sieur Vallentine! How pleased I am to see you again so soon!"

Vallentine turned to hear a familiar voice and his brow cleared of worry. Coming across the carpet to meet him was a good-looking young man, small of stature, with a head of tight black curls, dark expressive eyes, and a friendly smile.

"Cousin Hugh!? Now this is a pleasant surprise," Vallentine returned, and after the young man had executed a respectful bow, they shook hands. "What are you doin' in this hamlet? Last time we spoke you were tellin' Madame and me that you were returning to the provinces, and that tutorin' job—don't tell me! M'sieur de Chesnay's three boys. Fencin' and deportment—Am I wrong?"

The young man grinned, showing perfect white teeth. "No, sir. You are right. *Barnabé*, Benoîte, and Blaise."

Vallentine rolled his eyes and huffed. "Poor mites. I hope they have an aptitude for the sword, 'cause they're going to need it!"

"I am doing my best to provide them with those skills, sir," the young man replied and followed Vallentine across the room to a set of comfortable chairs and sofa arranged before a fireplace.

Here a footman had wheeled the morning tea trolley that had upon it the silver coffee urn, porcelain cups and plates, and a lavish assortment of delicacies that were as pleasing to the eye as they were mouth-watering.

Vallentine suddenly realised he was hungry. But spying the almond nougat from Montélimar he frowned and hesitated to fill his plate. Instead he poured out a dish of coffee and invited his guest to help himself and be comfortable on a wingchair.

"The youngest boy—Blaise—shows the most promise," the young man continued, as he set down his dish of coffee and plate that had upon it two small cream cakes and a piece of the *Nougat de Montélimar*, on a table by the wing chair. He then flicked aside the skirts of his blue wool frockcoat with large cuffs and silver buttons, to perch on the edge of a comfortable cushion, one booted leg forward, with foot turned out for anchorage.

"Good. He needs promise," Vallentine replied, impressed by the young man's elegant ease and a covetous eye on the nougat on his plate. He sipped his coffee. "Usually I'd have waited for our hostess before plunging into the morning tea trolley. But I've come to realise that when an infant's involved, there's no predictin' the whens or the wherefores."

"I fear what you say is true, sir. Two of my four sisters have children, so I have a little knowledge of such unpredictability."

"I'm sure they are devoted mothers. And without the burden of raisin' a precious ducal infant, I'll wager!"

The young man shook his head and was serious. "They are wives of provincial gentlemen. But I do not doubt that whether they are provincial or ducal-bred, all infants are precious to their parents, yes?"

"Yes! Yes! Of course," Vallentine blustered, suddenly ill at ease for speaking so frankly, and to a young man whom he had met only twice before—once in his wife's drawing room, and a second time at a renowned fencing academy in the city where he had helped him with a number of technical points in his swordplay.

"I do hope Mme la Duchesse can find the time to make my acquaintance," the young man stated conversationally in the protracted silence. "On the occasions I have called on Madame Vallentine, Mme la Duchesse d'Roxton has not been at home… Perhaps today will be different…?"

When Vallentine remained silent, the young man turned his attention to the assortment of cakes on his plate and drank his coffee.

"Are you the only one here?" His Lordship suddenly blurted out, a deep crease between his brows.

"I beg your pardon, sir?"

"Was anyone else shown into this room and left before I came in?"

"No, sir."

Vallentine's frown deepened. "Why are you here, Cousin Hugh?"

"To make the acquaintance of Mme la Duchesse, and because you invited me, sir."

"I invite—what?" Vallentine sat up and put aside his empty coffee dish. "I invited you? When, and who said so? Forgive me if I've startled you, but I'm fairly startled m'self!"

The young man also set aside his dish, and the plate, which had upon it an uneaten piece of almond nougat. "My cousin—Madame your wife—she sent a note to my lodgings with the invitation."

"Did she indeed? What did this invitation say?"

"It invited me to meet you here, on this day, at this prearranged hour—"

"Why?"

"You offered to accompany me to *La Grande Écurie*."

"Why would I do that?"

The young man was confused. "Pardon, sir, but when we last spoke, I told you of my desire to obtain employment at the fencing school within *La Grande Écurie*. And then upon another occasion, when I called upon Madame and you were absent, I mentioned to her that I had lodged an application with my credentials, and several letters of recommendation, one is from the Marquis de Chesnay, with the relevant authorities within *La Grande Écurie*—"

"And my wife offered that I'd put in a good word for you?"

When the young man nodded hopefully, Vallentine clicked his tongue and returned his nod with a thin smile. He knew when had been bested, and when there was no point pushing back against the *force majeure* of his wife combined with that of his sister-in-law. And he wasn't as ignorant now as when he had first entered the room. His memory, and the pieces of the puzzle were all fitting nicely together.

"Very well then," he added as he eased himself out of the wingchair. "I'd best stick to her word."

And as he stood, he leaned over and swiped the piece of *Nougat de Montélimar* left on the young man's discarded plate, and popped it into his mouth with an immense satisfaction. Just as he did so, a footman opened the door to admit one of the Duchess's ladies. She came straight up to him and dropped a curtsy.

"Don't tell me," Vallentine stated flatly, a finger in his mouth to dislodge the sticky blob of almond nougat from a back tooth. "Mme la Duchesse is unavoidably detained and won't now be joinin' us?"

"Yes, my lord. His little lordship will not settle and so Mme la Duchesse sends her apologies."

"That's probably for the best," Vallentine stated stoically. He smiled thinly at the young man and then stared straight at Antonia's lady-in-waiting. "She'll have less explainin' to do with M'sieur le Duc. As for me—well! That remains to be seen. You can let the Duchess know our guest and I went off to *La Grande Écurie* as planned. I hope to return in time for dinner. That's *if* I'm let inside the house once the Duke comes to hear of this—this—whatever *this* is! Off you go!"

He went to the tea trolley, took another piece of almond nougat and put it in his waistcoat pocket, then signalled for the young man to follow him out of the room. In the expansive foyer he called for his greatcoat and gloves.

"Left your sword with the porter, did you?"

"Yes, sir. I brought three blades with me," the young man volunteered. "I thought I might need them at *La Grande Écurie*, if called upon to demonstrate my prowess."

"Wise. And if your wrist and footwork are half as good as they were on the day we crossed swords, then the fencing school at *La Grande Écurie* would have to be mad not to admit you."

The young man was suddenly bashful. "I mean no disrespect, sir, but even you know, as an English nobleman, there is more to admittance than my fencing ability. You are considered the best swordsman on either side of the Channel, and yet you are not a member of *L'Majesty's La Grande Écurie*."

"I'm not a Frenchman."

"Neither is M'sieur le Duc d'Roxton, and yet he is a member, and M'sieur de Chesnay says M'sieur le Duc is also one of the *Secret du Roi*—"

Mention of the King's highly selective and clandestine diplomatic clique, that was an open secret amongst those in the know, but was most definitely not spoken of publicly, had Vallentine angrily interrupting the young man.

"Stop there," he cut in through his teeth. Now in his great coat and gloves, he stepped up to his guest and said quietly, so only he could hear, "Has no one told you it ain't wise to say aloud what is not spoken of except behind closed doors? Besides, you're bein' disrespectful, and in the nobleman's house no less." He stared down into the dark eyes that were suddenly startled and wary. "I'm an amiable fellow most of the time, but overstep good manners and that amiability is out the window. Understand, me?"

"Yes, sir. I apologise, sir. I only meant—"

"I don't care what you meant. And neither will M'sieur le Duc d'Roxton. And I am very sure you are aware of his reputation and of what he is capable. So I don't need to say it, but I will: Where his honor and his family are concerned, he counts no cost. You understand what I'm gettin' at?" When the young man nodded, Vallentine smiled grimly. "Then we understand one another. And you can take this back to de Chesnay: He's to stop bandyin' about M'sieur le Duc's name, in any situation, or he'll hear from me. Got it?"

"Yes, sir. Perfectly."

"And you'd best understand somethin' else before we head off, so you don't get any false expectations: Whatever it is you are hopin' to gain by your visits to my wife, or by your association with me, it will have no bearing on the outcome of your bid to gain the favor of Madame la Duchesse d'Roxton, and through her M'sieur le Duc d'Roxton. As long as you are reconciled to that, I am perfectly willing to be your mentor. I may not be a member of *La Grande Écurie*, but I'd wager my firstborn that to a man they hold me and my word in the highest esteem."

"Yes, sir. They do. I do. *Everyone* does! And not another word will I say about M'sieur le Duc. My word on it!"

"Then we'll have a pleasant enough afternoon, won't we?"

"Yes, sir. I hope so, sir. Crossing swords with you, learning from your swordplay, has been one of the great joys of my short life."

"That's the way! Keep it friendly, and keep it all about the sword, and we'll get on famously," Vallentine declared, a hand clapped a little too forcefully to the young man's shoulder so that it dipped under pressure.

And when they had stepped out of the house into the winter sunshine of the avenue all the uncharacteristic frostiness in Vallentine's manner evaporated, so that he was able to say to the young man without rancour,

"I don't know whose idea it was for you to style yourself Cousin Hugh—my wife's or that snivellin' insect, your cousin who shall not be named—but I give you full marks for honesty in frontin' up here and proffering your visitin' card. But if it's all the same to you, I'm goin' to drop callin' you Cousin Hugh and address you as Montbelliard, which is a better fit. *Allons-y!*"

By the time Vallentine returned to the villa, it was well past the dinner hour and so he presumed his hosts had retired for the evening. This suited His Lordship. He had ended up spending the entire day at *La Grande Écurie*, where he was greeted with much fanfare. And as soon as the teachers became aware just who was in their midst, regular classes were suspended and the students eagerly herded into the open theatre to watch and learn from a master in the art of swordsmanship.

There was none better than Lord Vallentine in the use of the épée. His posture, his footwork, and his attacking and parrying methods, were all second to none. And his execution of the riposte after a parry was greeted with gasps from some and applause by everyone. Keen students volunteered to be His Lordship's opponent in demonstrations. Several students who considered themselves experts, and as much younger men, able to best His Lordship in fitness if not in skill, were quickly dispatched. They were either outwitted at the strategic placement of the point of Vallentine's sword, or were sent all over the field of play by His Lordship's unrelenting thrust and parry, and were exhausted into submission.

At the end of the public demonstrations, Vallentine agreed to put through their paces the most promising of *La Grande Écurie's* young swordsmen. And true to his word, he included the Chevalier Montbelliard in all his discussions and demonstrations, putting the young man forward when he thought it appropriate, so that he came to the attention of the school's masters and most influential students. The Chevalier did his mentor proud by proving to be an excellent swordsman. What he lacked in height and length of thrust, he more than made up for in his quick-thinking swordplay and strategic placement of his point. So impressed were the masters that when it came time for the evening meal, not only His Lordship but also his protégé was given an invitation, and gratefully accepted.

All in all, Vallentine had a most pleasant day. He had managed to get in a few hours of exercise amongst his peers, and execute his promise to the Chevalier Montbelliard by bringing him to the attention of *La Grande Écurie's* fencing masters. He could do no more for the young man, and all that he had done should satisfy his wife and hopefully not find disfavour with his best friend.

He was about to slip between the bedcovers when he noticed the silver salver on the coverlet near his pillow. It had obviously been put there so he could not miss it. On the salver was a small rectangular card. Written on it in a hand he knew as well as his own were seven words: *Eight. The stable courtyard. Bring your sword.*

There was nothing odd in this. He and Roxton regularly engaged in fencing practice in the early morning. It was only when he turned the card over that he had an immediate obstruction in his throat and a hollow feeling in the pit of his stomach. Roxton had written on the back of the Chevalier's visiting card. Vallentine did not doubt he had done so deliberately; the Duke knew about the young man's visit to his villa, and if he knew that, then he knew the rest.

It was as well the day had left Vallentine exhausted or he would have tossed about all night. As it turned out, he fell into a deep sleep, one punctuated with dreams that made no sense but which left him with foreboding.

TEN

V ALLENTINE WAS mistaken in thinking that just because he
had returned in darkness to be greeted by the night porter
in a softly lit entrance foyer, that his hosts had retired for the
evening. That was far from the case. While an eerie silence had
descended upon the rest of the villa, with candles snuffed in rooms
not being used, light and laughter behind the doors of the Duke
and Duchess's apartment told a different tale.

AFTER A FULL DAY of hunting with the King, the Duke went
straight from the stables to his dressing closet and into his bath.
He was a keen horseman who enjoyed the thrill of the chase, and
was known for his endurance in the saddle, but once the ride or
the hunt was over, so was his desire to remain a moment longer
than was necessary in his riding attire. He was always impatient to
return to his customary sartorial splendor. The need to scrub off
the day's exertions, to be clean from head to foot, to wear fresh

linen, and clothing befitting his rank, became of paramount importance.

It was his grandfather, the fourth duke, who had instilled in him this requisite for cleanliness—that a nobleman's corporeal being must be scrubbed clean, and wear clean linens at all times, to be deserving of the sumptuous clothing befitting his august rank. Cleanliness in body and clothing were the outward manifestations of a nobleman's bloodline, and the cornerstone of his character. Without a spotless person, nothing else could follow. It set noble apart from peasant. And the only way to know the difference between the two was to experience the latter to appreciate the former.

To prove his point the fourth duke had forced his grandson to live in his own filth for the first several months under his jurisdiction. The boy had limited access to fresh water, was forbidden adequate sanitation, and was made to wear the linens and suit of clothes he had arrived in from France. It took six months, but the old duke achieved his object. For the rest of his life his grandson had an obsession with cleanliness.

The Duke never went a day without scrubbing his body clean, changing his linens, and wearing clothing that was spotless. It was said he had the most assiduous and well-paid laundrymaids in all Europe.

After the hunt he always sent an outrider on ahead to alert his household to prepare for his return. His dedicated retinue went into action to ensure there was plenty of hot water to draw his bath, that his shaving implements were sharpened, and clean linens and several articles of clothing were set out for him to choose from. If he required sustenance, this was communicated to his cook, and if there were letters that had arrived during his absence, these were set on his dressing table ready for his attention after he had bathed and been dressed.

It was at the shaving stage that his valet usually provided him with any further news considered relevant. But as Martin Ellicott was away on business in Paris, it fell to one of the under-valets to take on this task. With the Duke seated at his dressing table the under-valet made him aware of certain particulars within his household.

Two items were of special note: The visiting card atop the pile of correspondence which identified Lord Vallentine's morning caller, and the verbal conflagration in the kitchen involving the pastry chef. Jean-Camille made it known to anyone who was listening—and those who were not could not help over-hearing—that he was employed to provide M'sieur le Duc with the most mouth-watering delicious desserts and macarons in all France. He was not there to feed the dull palates of the house-hold rabble. By which he meant, so the nervous under-valet explained when the Duke put up his brows, Jean-Camille had become enraged when he discovered his macarons had been distributed amongst the servants, principally the laundresses and the nursery maids.

The Duke did not comment about his temperamental pastry chef and showed only mild interest in the visiting card. He went on to open and read the several letters awaiting him on a tray. But he returned to the visiting card, peering at it through his quizzing glass before expertly passing it through the long, tapered fingers of one hand—as one does a playing card when performing a trick for the entertainment of elderly aunts and wide-eyed children—while the attendant related to him how the card of the Chevalier Mont-belliard came to be in the villa.

Inscrutable as ever, the Duke then called for quill and ink, wrote on the back of the card and then instructed to whom it was to be delivered, and how.

Satisfied with his appearance, he slipped his long feet into a pair of red leather Moroccan mules, and shrugged a banyan of exquisitely painted silk over a crisp white shirt, silver thread waist-coat, and pair of black velvet breeches. He put his quizzing glass and letters in a pocket and went in search of his duchess.

ANTONIA WAS CURLED up in the window seat of their sitting room, reading. The last traces of winter light shone through the window over her shoulder, but candles burning in their sconces above her head and across the room meant there was plenty of light. And with her knees drawn up to balance a large, heavy volume in her lap, and absently twirling a long lock of her fair hair, all her concentration was on the printed page. That there was a pile of books at her stockinged feet, and several more open on the carpet with ribbons to hold a place, meant that she had possibly managed to spend a few hours in her favorite pastime in quiet solitude, or so the Duke hoped.

He did not wish to interrupt her, so leaned a shoulder in the doorway and waited, taking the opportunity to admire her lovely profile in silhouette against the setting sun. Her beauty made his throat dry, and in these small, quiet moments, when he thought about providence—that this sweet creature was indeed his wife— his heart beat that little bit faster. But what never failed to make him in awe of his good fortune was her unselfconscious delight every time they were reunited, even if they had only been apart from each other for a few hours.

He knew well the book she was reading: Livy's *Histories* translated from the Latin into English by the scholar Philemon Holland. He had recently had it rebound in leather, and he had recommended it to her when she had expressed an interest in knowing more about the Punic Wars. It was one of a dozen books brought with her from the hotel, but this one she had devoted more time, intent on wading through the Elizabethan English.

He noted that in amongst the books strewn on the carpet there were a pair of discarded mules, the remnants of an afternoon tea, a baby's white woollen blanket, and an infant's single stocking. He would have been surprised had there not been evidence of their infant son's presence. The absence of a cradle meant she was at least adhering to their new regimen. And then he saw that she was using their son's other stocking as a place holder. Trust her to repurpose such an article of clothing! His shoulders shook and he chuckled.

At once Antonia looked up, and all the concentration left her face. In its place was a dazzling smile. She shut the book with a clap, and put it aside.

"Monseigneur! Renard! Why did you not tell me you were here?" Antonia scolded playfully, rushing over to him to be gathered up in his arms. Her green eyes went very round. "Do you know that today is the longest we have been apart since our marriage? I know it is only a day, and not a whole day, but it truly feels like a sennight!"

He grinned and then looked thoughtful. "A week? Perhaps I shall not hunt again with the King."

"Not hunt with the King?" Antonia repeated with a gasp. And then she chuckled and snuggled in. "You are teasing me! Of course you must hunt with the King. You enjoy each other's company. Besides, you are a great huntsman and there is none better to match you in the saddle but the King."

"His Majesty might view it differently. That I am a match for *his* skill as rider and huntsman. One does not best a king, in anything, if one can help it. It is not—er—politic."

Antonia was nonplussed. "But—Renard, that must be very difficult for you, to be less than your best, and yet appear as if you are giving of your best, yes? And even more so with a king."

"Never a truer word spoken," he agreed, carrying her back over the low window seat. Here he set her down, standing on the cushions. She was almost at eye-level now, and when she rested her hands on his shoulders to anchor herself, he added, "How is it you understand at once what I have tried to explain to Vallentine a dozen times or more?"

"Oh, that is simple," she said with a shrug, yet her eyes sparkled with mischief. "Vallentine, he knows you, but not as I do.

He is very open about everything, which is commendable. It is one of the reasons you like him, yes? But you…" Her smile became wistful. "You do not like to be open about anything with anyone —except with me."

"You are the exception—in every particular."

"That pleases me very much. It is how it will always be between us."

"Always." He looked into her eyes. "May I kiss you?"

She smiled. "Please. I have been waiting for you to do so."

They shared a long, lingering kiss, and when they next spoke, they were comfortably seated amongst the cushions.

The Duke asked, "Were you as surprised as I that His Majesty chose to come to the villa to collect me?"

"Very. It is a great honor, is it not, for the King to do so?"

"Yes. But what is most important is that it brings us one step closer to your recognition at Court, *mignonne.*"

Antonia pondered. "In all the time I was living at the palace with *Grandpère,* never was I as near to His Majesty as I was this morning at the gallery windows. He is always surrounded by a great crush of courtiers and his Swiss, that only a child sitting on his father's shoulders would be able to see him at all clearly. It must be tiresome for him to be stared at and surrounded all the time, do you not think?"

"One of the more tiring consequences of being king. Which is why he jealously guards his privacy and his friendships. In private he is able to be himself."

"He is not unlike you in that way."

He kissed the back of her hand and smiled. "You will see for yourself when I take you with me to one of his little suppers."

Antonia glanced at him sideways, an impish smile hovering about her lovely mouth.

"And at this supper, I will be able to better judge if His Majesty is as handsome as he is looking down at him from our window."

The Duke was not fooled but he played along. He raised an eyebrow. "Need I be worried?"

"Of Louis?" Antonia gave what she hoped was a nonchalant shrug. "The courtiers and the ladies they do not lie. They are not flatterers, when they say he is the handsomest man in all France. And yet—"

"Yet?"

"—you are more *arrestingly* handsome."

"I am glad to hear my wife say so."

"And—"

The Duke pretended to be surprised. "There is a condition attached?"

"—I do not desire him, only you."

He squeezed her fingers. "The perfect wifely response to assuage a husband's dignity."

"But I am not at all dignified, Renard," Antonia confessed. "I have the most undignified thoughts when you are dressed *en désha-billé* as you are now."

The Duke was nonplussed. "You do, *ma chérie*? This banyan pleases you?"

"Oh, it pleases me very much!" Antonia could not keep up her solemnity for long, and she hunched her shoulders and leaned in to kiss him. "I confess that when you are dressed in this way, I just want to run my hands all over your body and strip you out of your clothes!"

Her admission was so unaffected that to his amazement the Duke felt his face warm. Antonia saw it too and misconstrued his response.

"I have embarrassed you."

"Not at all. It's just—I can't recall a time when I have blushed before. And yet you have made me do so with one fell swoop of your carnal honesty."

She looked into his dark eyes.

"But it is the truth. What you do with your body—to me and

with me—and how you make me feel, it is—it is *au-delà du bonheur*. It is the same for you?"

"*Ma fée*, that you need ask," he replied gently and kissed her forehead.

Antonia drew herself up and put her arms about his neck. She looked at him from under her lashes, head cocked to the side, and asked with deceptive sweetness, "Monseigneur, would it be very wicked of us to make love on this window seat?"

"No. It would be—" The Duke grinned and pulled her against him. "—*wonderfully* wicked."

ELEVEN

THE DUKE and Duchess had their evening meal served to them at the small table by the fireplace, both dressed *en déshabillé* in silk banyans, damp disorderly curls scraped back with silk ribbons to provide some semblance of decorum. Yet when they glanced across the silver at each other, Antonia smiled into her napkin and the Duke into his wine glass. Both had the same thought—that they had not been very decorous earlier, succumbing to their desires by making love on the window seat, and then bathing together. And in amongst the soap bubbles by an open fire, they discussed what Antonia had read earlier that afternoon about the differing attitudes of the Romans and the Carthaginians to empire, until the bathwater went tepid.

And now they were doing their best to restore their ducal dignity with a formal dinner, servants padding back and forth with the culinary delights created by the Duke's renowned Parisian chef André. Their conversation was mostly about the letters the Duke had received from England, which were open beside his plate. And there was one piece of news he knew would please Antonia as much as it did him. It was from the kennel master at Treat and concerned his beloved whippets.

He couldn't help smiling when he told her, "Samuels informs me Tan is the proud sire of five healthy pups, two dogs and three bitches. All are doing very well indeed."

Antonia clapped her hands. "*Cette nouvelle me rend très heureuse*! Oh! Renard! That is such wonderful news! Does this mean we will soon be reunited with Tan and Raf?"

"Soon. Raf has a few more months of training with Tan. Their trainer—John? Yes, John—will accompany both to Paris. Possibly in time for Christmas."

"I hope it is so. I am exceedingly impatient for them to be with us." She glanced at the letters by his plate. "Tan having a new companion in Raf must surely be helping him recover from the loss of Gray?"

"I daresay it has."

"And you, *mon cher*?" she asked gently. "Has it helped you?"

The Duke paused for a moment, wine glass in mid-air. He then took a sip, and setting down the glass, looked across at Antonia and held her gaze.

"No one ever fully recovers from the loss of a faithful companion, particularly when that companion is so callously taken. But you know that. You must also know, *mignonne*, that I will never forget, nor can I forgive that I came within a whisker of losing you and Julian, too. That remains an open wound, one that can never heal, not until that malignant blot on our lives breathes his last."

Antonia nodded her understanding, knowing the malignant blot was the Comte de Salvan, and said no more. She was fully prepared for him to ask her about the visit of the Comte's heir, the Chevalier Montbelliard, because she was certain he knew all about it. But when he did not, she was relieved. And then the moment passed when a footman enquired where they would prefer to have their coffee.

The Duke deferred to Antonia, and she chose their sitting

room and the low table where the backgammon board was set up for play. Yet when the footman lingered, the Duke and Duchess exchanged a look, and the Duke waved a hand for the man to speak.

"Jean-Camille sends his apologies, and regrets to inform M'sieur le Duc that there are no macarons to accompany the coffee this evening."

"None?" the Duke asked, putting aside his napkin to stand. "Not one—"

"It is of no importance," Antonia interrupted airily. "Coffee is all we require."

The Duke regarded his wife with surprise. Although her quick reply brought a spark of memory of what his under-valet had told him earlier about a verbal conflagration in the kitchen involving his pastry chef. He decided to test an assumption.

"You are not disappointed that our house is devoid of macarons, *ma vie?*"

She took hold of his hand and led him away from the table towards the *enfilade*.

"I assure you I am all devastation, Monseigneur, but we can look forward to macarons tomorrow night."

Roxton willingly let her guide him across the room and down the *enfilade* to the sitting room. He was mentally grinning when he teased her by appearing oblivious to the reason why there were no sweets to have with coffee.

"But, *ma chérie*... I do not doubt Jean-Camille will whip us up a new batch of macarons and other sweet delicacies to have with tomorrow's coffee. What remains a mystery is the whereabouts of today's batch. Perhaps I should summon Madame Ballon—"

"No. There is no need to do that."

"Oh? You think our housekeeper has no idea what—"

Now in the sitting room, Antonia let go of his hand and faced him with a pout.

"You are teasing me! And I know you are teasing me because

you cannot disguise from me the laughter in your voice. I hear the inflection at the end of the words where you try to hide your mirth. But you cannot hide this from me. And so there it is," she added with a grumble. "I have told you my secret of knowing when you are being a tease—though I know Vallentine and Madame seem not to be aware, which amazes me—and now I have lost the advantage. That you know means you might not do it again—"

He pulled her into his arms. "I will. For you. I *was* teasing you. And Vallentine and my sister remain deaf to it because they are not you. But something else—or someone—is bothering you…?"

"I am sorry for being ill-humored. And you are right. Vallentine he said something *about* me—not *to* me. It is a silly thing and Vallentine he is not to blame, so you must not scold him. Let us play at backgammon, and that will surely put me in a better mood."

She moved out of his arms and kicked off her silk mules to curl up amongst the cushions, the Duke placing the backgammon board between them. They were well into their first game when Antonia broke the comfortable silence between them by blurting out a confessional.

"I sent all the macarons to the laundry."

The Duke paused in throwing his dice. He did not look up from the state of play. "The—er—laundry, *ma vie?*"

"For the laundresses who spend all day amongst the suds."

The Duke captured one of Antonia's pieces and took it off the board. He glanced up.

"You think the food and lodging, not to mention monetary remuneration, provided to the laundresses is sadly lacking, and we must feed them our macarons, too?"

Antonia threw dice that made a combination which allowed her to return her captured pieces to the inner table. The Duke threw a double six, and the game continued.

"As to that I could not say," Antonia said. "But you have a

steward and a housekeeper at each house, so they can tell you, yes?"

"Each of our houses has a housekeeper, but I keep only two stewards," the Duke explained. "One here in Paris, and another at the family seat at Treat. It is their function to do everything necessary to ensure our comfort. Which I am happy to report they excel, or they would not be in my employ. The—er—trifling details with which I need not concern myself I leave to them."

"And macarons are a trifling detail, Monseigneur?"

"Their creation, yes. As to their distribution…? I am certain my housekeepers and stewards are in accord with me."

"Which is?"

Such was Antonia's studious expression that it took all the Duke's willpower to keep his features impassive. "I would counsel against supplying macarons to the laundry maids on a regular basis. Such vital work as they do cannot be sustained by sweets alone."

Antonia chuckled and said without rancour as she moved her pieces out of reach of capture, "You are being droll! I sent the macarons not to sustain them, but on a whim. There was so much left on the plates after Vallentine's morning tea with—which is why I offered the macarons where I thought they would be most appreciated," she continued smoothly, mentally sighing her relief she had again not mentioned the Chevalier Montbelliard. "It was a gesture—I wanted them to know that we do not forget all that laundresses do for us."

"Your thoughtfulness humbles me."

Antonia scooped up her dice and looked at the Duke.

"But think of it, Renard," she said earnestly. "They have taken on so much more washing and cleaning and ironing since Julian's arrival."

"I would rather not think about it."

"To be truthful, it is not something I wish to do either," Antonia confessed. "But I must because although I am your duchess, I am also Julian's mother. And as his mother I am truly grateful I do not have to do all that the laundresses and nursemaids do to care for our son. Do you not sometimes wonder if they are happy doing it, because I wonder, and I know I would not be happy in the least. And neither would you."

The Duke pulled a face of revulsion which made Antonia giggle.

"No. I would not! I cannot imagine anyone being—er—*happy* cleaning up after an infant, least of all dealing with the mountains of laundry one tiny being generates every day. Thank you for bringing this to my attention, *ma chérie*."

"You are most welcome, *mon amour*," Antonia replied sweetly.

She watched the Duke bear off the last of his pieces to win the first game and then eagerly reset the board for a chance to level the score.

"It is not only what is truly involved in cleaning Julian's linens that had me wondering about the laundresses," she explained. "But also all those who are necessary to our comfort. I do not want unhappy servants in our houses. And I do not only mean our personal servants, Renard, but the ones I—we—do not see at all."

"Wanting for everyone's happiness is commendable, *mignonne*. But that may not be possible. I can only speak from the experience of our own kind, but I am sure you realise that there are people in this world, regardless of their situation, who are unsatisfied with everything and everyone—"

"*Grand-mère* she is one such as that. I have never known anyone to be as miserable and as mean without reason as she. I was unhappy living with her because of it."

The Duke looked up from putting his pieces in place. There was a note of anger in his tone, anger directed at himself. "That was not entirely her fault. I take my share of the blame for what you went through under her roof."

"You suffer regret. She does not allow herself to feel the slightest regret, about anything!" Antonia's green eyes went wide.

"Monseigneur, can you imagine being a servant in her household!?"

"It is not a—er—place I wish to take my imagination… And you, *ma lutine*, cannot take the sins of all masters upon your lovely shoulders."

"You think me naïve."

"No. What I do think is that your infinite capacity to put yourself in the shoes of others may upon occasion lead you—er—astray."

Antonia cocked her head and frowned in thought. "Vallentine he tells me that as I am a duchess, I must now keep a proper distance from the servants. I know Madame she does not approve of my visits below stairs. But the servants are always welcoming. But now I am your duchess, am I not permitted to do this anymore? And if not, how am I to know what is happening below stairs, and if our servants they are happy in our houses—if I do not see them for myself?"

"I understand your predicament, *ma belle*, and I can help you understand it by presenting it to you in another way."

"Please do, because me I am very confused by it all."

The Duke suppressed the desire to grin and kept a perfectly straight face, because he admired her studious concern and did not want her to think him disingenuous.

"When you visited my kitchens as Mlle Moran it was not considered an—er—intrusion. Your visits were a welcome distraction in the daily routine of my servants, and they no doubt were pleased that you showed an interest in their work, and in them. I would also venture to add that who would not welcome a visit from you, who bring sunshine to everyone's day?"

"Ah! You pay me the loveliest compliments, Monseigneur!" Antonia beamed, and snatched up his fingers to kiss the back of his hand. "Thank you."

"Do not thank me, *ma vie*. I was stating fact. But to explain my sister's—er—concerns… By the by," he said, tweaking one of her long curls come loose and dangling over a shoulder. "I do not believe Vallentine would have given this matter one second of his consideration had he been left to his own thoughts—"

"But he is a loyal husband. And as Madame is upset by my visits to the kitchen, he Vallentine does not like to see his wife upset."

"Just so. He is to be commended for that. But there are times, times such as this, when it would be beneficial for him to keep his opinions to himself. It is not his place to comment on what you do, how you do it, when, or where. You are my duchess, and so the matter—any matter—is of concern to no one but me."

"And so, *you* would prefer I not visit the kitchens, or send macarons to the laundresses, or speak with the servants?"

"It is not a question of what I want," the Duke replied gently, hearing the wounded tone in her question.

"But—Monseigneur! I find that very hard to believe. Surely since you succeeded your *grand-père* to the title, your life it has always been about what you want."

The Duke blinked and then let out an involuntary bark of laughter at the simple truth in her statement.

"That is very true, *ma fée*. After all," he added on a teasing drawl, "dukes are by the very nature of their birth and title the natural benefactors of respect and—er—veneration. Some, like me, more than others. And so we do as we please and get what we please, when it pleases us."

Antonia ignored his banter, nor did she see anything surprising in what he said, because she believed it about him. But she did not believe it about his grandfather.

"But the fourth duke, he was not deserving of such respect, was he? He was heartless and cruel. He snatched you away from your mother when you were only a boy, a boy who had lost one parent, and now had no parents at all, and—"

"Dear me!" Roxton drawled, a sudden flush to his cheeks. "No guesses as to the source of these tales."

"But they are not tales, are they?" Antonia persisted stubbornly. "It is the truth. I am sorry, Renard. But what happened to you as a boy it upsets me, and perhaps more than such tales usually would because—because we now have an infant. I could no more let Julian be taken from me as stop breathing!"

"Come here, *ma vie*," he coaxed, and moved the backgammon board that was between them. And when she snuggled in, he held her in a comforting embrace. "That is a circumstance you never need concern yourself with," he assured her. "As for my—er—lamentable boyhood… I will give you a proper account of those sad events someday—"

"Promise?"

"I do, but let us not spoil this lovely evening alone with talk of the fourth duke. And if that makes me a selfish duke, then so be it."

Antonia sighed her contentment. "We are well matched. I am a selfish duchess. I love having you all to myself."

He kissed her hair, and they stayed that way on the chaise longue, quiet and still and enjoying the moment, hoping it would go on forever. It lasted less than five minutes.

Without warning, and the usual padding in of a footman to announce in dulcet tones an interruption to their solitude, one of the Morvan wet nurses with two nursery maids at her back, swept into the sitting room unannounced. There was no need for explanations. The loud lusty cries of an infant with hunger pangs told the ducal couple everything they needed to know.

Without so much as a word or a look, the Duke vacated the chaise longue and left the room. He knew when to beat a retreat. But he did not abandon Antonia for long. He returned a little while later, when tranquillity was restored to the sitting room, a footman on his heels carrying a tray of fresh coffee things. He placed the backgammon board back on the chaise and looked across at his wife with a smile.

"Where were we?"

TWELVE

Antonia accepted the cup of coffee the Duke made for her, a glance down at her infant, who was suckling contentedly, chubby fingers anchored in the folds of her silk banyan.

"I am constantly amazed what a difference a few minutes make to him," Antonia confessed. "One minute he is a bawling red mess, and now look! The happiest baby in all the world."

The Duke sipped at his coffee. "That surprises you?" he drawled, one eyebrow raised. "He is in the happiest place in all the world."

Antonia chuckled. He smiled and winked. And they drank their coffee in companionable silence, gaze on their infant. When the Duke took her empty cup away, she said with a small sigh,

"Monseigneur, I love him beyond words. He is the most perfect infant in all the world—"

"Of course. He is ours."

"—but would it shock you if I confessed that while he is on the breast, I am longing to do something, anything else, but sit here like this? And then I feel guilty for my impatience."

"Understandable on both counts. I am very sure all mothers

continually feel guilty about something to do with their offspring. And while he feeds you are his—er—captive, are you not?"

Antonia thought about this a moment and then nodded. "That is very true… Do you know there are mothers who are able to get on with their day and not feel guilty, because they must. They do not have the luxury I do, so I truly should not complain, should I?"

"Are you complaining? I thought you were merely unnecessarily castigating yourself. Unwarranted, by the way."

"Thank you for saying so." Antonia regarded her son with a soft smile as she lightly stroked his mop of dark hair. "Perhaps if he sees me reading, he will like to read too?"

"How can he not?"

Antonia looked up at the Duke. "I did not know this but perhaps you did: Céleste she tells me there are women who work in the field who feed their infant while they work."

"You amaze me."

"It is true—"

"I believe you, *ma vie*. I am amazed."

"Oh! I see… What these women of the field do is wear a sling across their bodies, and they put their infant into the sling and on the breast. And there they remain content so their mothers can continue doing whatever it is they are doing in the field."

"What infant would not be content, warm against their mother, and with access to what he most wants at all times? You are telling me this because you would like to do this?" the Duke asked with a perfectly straight face. "My only question is: What—er—work in the field do you wish to take up?"

"Renard, if I had a cushion to hand, I would throw it at you!"

The Duke grinned. "Shall I pass you one, *ma lutine*?"

Antonia stuck out her bottom lip and feigned brooding annoyance. And when the Duke mimicked her, she could not continue with her deception and she chuckled. He leaned in and kissed her forehead.

"Speaking of *lavoratori dei campi,* or more precisely *lavoratori in cucina*," he said conversationally, an arm resting along the back of the chaise. "You asked earlier about what it was about your visits to the kitchen as *la mia duchessa* that made them different from when you visited as *Signorina* Moran, and why *mia sorella* has taken it upon herself to make her disapproval known."

Antonia's eyes widened and a glance over her shoulder was indication she knew precisely why he had chosen to converse with her in Italian—a language they both knew well—and not in her native French. The wet nurse and one of the nursery maids remained in the shadows waiting to attend to his little lordship and ready him for bed, once he had finished feeding.

That the Duke did not want their continuing conversation understood by their servants made Antonia acutely aware that she must have indeed transgressed unwritten rules within the household. And it was no wonder his sister and Vallentine were upset with her. But she was also philosophical. No one had told her these rules, so how did she know not to break them?

With his next words, the Duke seemed to read her mind. "I blame myself for not explaining matters to you earlier. But we were caught up in the impending birth, were we not? And what bothers Estée is insignificant in the greater scheme of our life, and could wait until after our son's arrival."

"And now it can no longer wait because Madame she is still unhappy with me for visiting the kitchens, and this is also now bothering you, too? I was prepared to be guided by her. It would be churlish of me, would it not, *monsignore*, not to be, because she has a vast experience of these domestic matters and I have none."

"You are too hard on yourself, *vita mia*. Besides," he added flatly, sitting back, "I do not care in the least if Estée's feelings are wounded. It is not her place to criticise how you conduct yourself as duchess. Truth told, it is her intolerable interference that has fanned the flames of resentment below stairs. This has caused unrest amongst the servants, and has become an unnecessary burden on my time."

"I understand your annoyance, but I am no closer to knowing what it is that offends Madame—and you."

"Me? Nothing you say or do offends me in the least, Antonia," he responded flatly, then added with a soft smile, "Except that you think I would be offended."

"Offends is too strong a word, mayhap. But I know you, and I know it bothers you that I go below stairs to visit your chefs, and ask to sample the biscuits and the sauces. You said so yourself that my capacity to wear the shoes of others has upon occasion led me astray—"

"*Infinite* capacity, *ma belle*."

"But I ask you, Renard, how else am I to learn to be a good duchess if I do not know how our households they are run, and what the servants in their own shoes do in their day-to-day lives. And we do not have one house but *three*. Four, if you wish to count this villa."

"We will be counting this villa from now on. So four."

"Is there another nobleman either side of the Channel who keeps *four* open houses, with enough servants inside and out to allow him to arrive on any given day as if he has never stepped away? None but you."

The Duke threw up a hand. "But, *gioia mia*, how we choose to live is of concern to no one but us, surely?"

"True, but how those households are run is very much your concern, and mine now, is it not?"

"It is," he replied, inclining his head. "But everything can wait until Julian's regimen is firmly in place, and after your presentation at Court—"

"No, Monsignore," Antonia stated firmly. "That we have an infant is no excuse for neglecting my responsibilities. And I am not so shallow-brained that I am only capable of focusing on my son and my presentation before the King." She smiled. "But I do love you so very much for making these excuses for me, but no more."

He took a few moments to respond, head leaning on his fist, content to watch and marvel at her, to marvel at them both. But mostly marvel at his wife, who while feeding her fourteen-week-old infant was worrying about her duties as his duchess. Which reminded him of the conversation he had had with Vallentine, that when he was her age, the last thing on his mind was his responsibilities, ducal or otherwise.

She had a small towel over a shoulder and had placed Julian against it, and was rubbing his tiny back in slow circular motions to settle his belly. And as he settled, he nestled into her neck and was slowly drifting off to sleep. Antonia sensed this and looked over her shoulder, signal for the wet nurse and maid to come forward and collect her son for the night. Before she handed him over to their care, she kissed his cheek and kissed him some more, telling him how much his mama and papa loved him but that it was time for him to sleep in his own bed. And off he went, secure in the arms of his nurse, and out of the sitting room, Antonia watching after him longingly.

The Duke knew that despite complying with the new regimen for their son's nightly feeds, and spending those nights with his night nurses in a cradle in the nursery gallery so she could sleep uninterrupted, Antonia would continue to fret. This was only natural, but he did his best to divert her.

"I have never visited the kitchens," he confessed, reverting to her native French. "Nor have I been below stairs. Were I to venture there I would most certainly become lost."

"Are you funning with me, Monseigneur?" Antonia asked, turning to stare at him and instantly attentive. When he shook his head she added, still incredulous, "You mean you have never been below stairs at this villa?"

"Any of my houses, not as Duke. And if I did visit the kitchen of the hotel as a boy, it was when I was still in skirts. So I have no memory of the occasion."

"I do not understand. You may venture anywhere you wish."

"I may but I choose not to."

"But how do you know what is happening there, or how the servants are being treated—No! That is naïve of me. Of course you know. Others tell you."

"Naturally I have the right to go anywhere I please. But I do not. Everyone has a place, even my esteemed self. I have made below stairs off limits to this duke. In that way, those who work there may get on with their day, and their lives, without fear of a visit or interference from me."

"And Madame, she does not venture there either?"

"She does not."

Antonia thought about this a moment. "I see that if you did visit below stairs, it would be disconcerting for the servants. Many would spend their time looking over their shoulder, wondering if you might appear at any moment—"

"—like a spectre?" Roxton smiled, liking the idea. "Perhaps I should reconsider my own maxim…"

"But Madame has lived at the hotel her whole life," Antonia continued, ignoring his caustic levity, "and so she knew your maxim that it is not her place to visit amongst servants. But I am not her, and I am not you—"

"*Mignonne*, do you not see that as my duchess you are an extension of me? Wherever you go, whatever you do, we are now forever linked as one."

Antonia smiled happily. "I like that. It gives me comfort."

"And me great joy. But to some, to those in our employ, when you choose to go below stairs, it is as if I have descended amongst them."

Antonia's green eyes widened with new knowledge. "Oh! I had not thought of it in that way."

"And as kind and as generous as your gesture was in sending

Jean-Camille's macarons to the laundry, he would have seen it differently. He, like André, and our cooks and chefs in England, take great pride in serving their ducal master. They can boast and complain and spend a great deal of their day berating their underlings because of whom they serve, having attached themselves to my consequence. But if their culinary creations end up in the mouths of laundresses—"

"—they cannot boast that they were favored by you?"

"And you, *ma vie*."

Antonia's shoulders sagged. "Then my kindness to the laundry maids was one big embarrassment for Jean-Camille?"

"Not necessarily. Most of the household will see your gesture for what it is. And those that do not and who attempt to torment Jean-Camille with this seeming fall from grace will get short shrift from Duvalier. And as this is the first—"

"—and last."

The Duke inclined his head. "—and last time Jean-Camille need face such a humiliation, the slight done his little delicacies will soon be forgotten."

Antonia smiled. "I will be sure to praise his macarons tomorrow night, and eat two."

"He will be over the moon." When Antonia's smile dropped and the crease was back between her brows he asked, "What is it, *ma fée*? You foresee a problem with this plan to restore Jean-Camille's pride?"

She shook her head. "No. It is as you say. It's just that if I am not to venture below stairs, how am I to know—to know—anything about the household and its running?"

The Duke took hold of her hand. "You told me the answer earlier. Others tell me. And those others are your eyes and ears also. Our housekeepers and butlers and upper servants, all of whom are in such positions because of their expertise and loyalty, are there to offer you their opinion and guidance. They will be only too pleased not to be overlooked by you."

"Is that how they see my visits to the kitchen? That I have overlooked them?"

"Can they see it any other way?"

Antonia fiddled with the silken cord of her banyan in thought, then confessed, looking up at the Duke. "I admit to being a little intimidated by such servants. They are skilled in what they do and have many years' experience, so how are they to take direction from one such as me who is young and know nothing?"

"Not that I believe that to be the case, but say for argument's sake that is so… You knew nothing when you were Mlle Moran; what has changed in a few months?"

"But now I am a duchess it is not acceptable for me to be ignorant, yes?" She smiled hesitantly, a twinkle in her eye. "When I was Mlle Moran, I did not know then that I did not know what I do not know now. *Tu comprends, mon cher mari?*"

The Duke nodded and gently cupped her face. "Antonia, all that matters to me is that you are happy as my duchess. All else can be learned or overcome. And you are welcome to put your own stamp on the position. There has not been a duchess of Roxton since my grandmother, and she passed away some thirty-six years ago. If you wish to reward lower servants for their services, then do so. But you will need to find a way without embarrassing the upper servants. I have every confidence in you doing so. But I do not deny that there will be times when you will find the position burdensome, when a great many expectations will be placed upon you, by family and servants alike. Unfortunately, you will have to do your best to bear it for the rest of *my* life."

"None of it is a burden as long as you are with me," she replied fiercely, turning her face into his hand to press her lips to his palm. She sat up with a smile. "And you are wrong, so wrong, Renard. I will be your duchess for all of *our lives*, in this life, and the next. Do you also believe that?"

"Yes," he stated without hesitation. "With all my heart. I

would not have thought it possible before you twirled into my life, but I do now."

Antonia threw her arms about his neck, and as she did so, the infant blanket that had been at her shoulder slipped down into her lap. It prompted a vivid memory from earlier in the day, when she was at the gallery window curtseying to the King. She pulled back and stared at the Duke, green eyes wide, mortified.

"Renard! I have had the most awful thought. This morning when I made my curtsey to Louis, and I was holding Julian in my arms… Was he…" She held up the baby blanket. "He was wearing a short shift and he had one of these wrapped around him because he had yet to be put into his clout and pilch. I turned him to the window, so you could see him and he you, and he was kicking his legs and squealing. It was if he was vocalizing the excitement the household was feeling that His Majesty was in the courtyard. It was so delightful a sound that I forgot all about the blanket… I think he kicked it off to the floor."

"That would explain it then."

"What? What does it explain? That I was holding Julian up so you could see him and there was His Majesty thinking I was showing him that here is proof I am the proud mother of a son?"

The Duke could not stifle a grin. "That's exactly what he thought, *ma vie*."

Antonia drew in a breath of surprise. "What did he say?"

"His Majesty remarked that he was delighted to see with his own eyes that the rumors of your great beauty are true."

Antonia dared to mimic the King of France. "Roxton, your duchess she is very beautiful. I can scarce believe my royal eyes at your great luck, my friend—"

"But Your Majesty," the Duke drawled as if speaking to the King, yet his shoulders shook with laughter. "I assure you that luck had nothing to do with—"

Antonia stopped him with a kiss, and she also stopped her mimicry to say indignantly, "It is not important if he thinks me a great beauty or not when he must also think me a great imbecile to do such a thing as to hold Julian up for his inspection!"

"*Ma vie*, I assure you His Majesty had no need to question your intelligence. Far from it. He in fact thought the opposite. He was impressed by your shrewdness."

Antonia sat back, scowling. "I do not understand why he would think what I did anything but the actions of a proud but very silly mother."

"You are correct in your assumption. His Majesty presumed you were holding up our infant to show him, and thus the world, proof you had indeed given me an heir. He was rather solemn, and gave the moment its due. And by raising his hat to you, with his companions looking on, he was acknowledging this proof and giving you his royal approval."

"Why would he go out of his way to do such a thing?"

"Because we—he and I—are friends."

"That is not in question surely? And if there were any question as to that, His Majesty did you the great honor of riding into the courtyard to greet you. And as you say, with the princes and noblemen looking on from the park." She regarded the Duke keenly. "There is something else—something you are not telling me."

Roxton brushed an imaginary crease from his silken knee. His tone was flat.

"There is. You know that I have—er—attracted enemies over the years. As a consequence, there are rumors concerning my esteemed self, some of which are true, others sordid, most baseless. I do not usually concern myself, and you need not hear about them. But there is one that has become persistent, and I will not allow it to fester. I tell you only because it will explain the King's response to your quite innocent action this morning. We married in the February, and Julian he was born in the July. There is a—er—discrepancy in the timeline of his gestation and birth. This has caused scurrilous questions to circulate court, one of which asks then if he is indeed my son and not—"

"No! That is too silly for words!" Antonia interrupted, indignant and dismissive. And when she hopped off the chaise, he stood too. "Anyone with working eyes has only to look at Julian to see you are his sire."

The Duke's frown lifted and he smiled down at her. "But most —er—working eyes have not seen our son, *mignonne*. Hence the rumor. And spread about by some of the very noblemen who were watching on when Louis lifted his tricorne."

"And now they too have seen Julian for themselves," Antonia replied with a sweet smug smile. "I am glad you did not tell me before now. And I am grateful to His Majesty for the gesture of acknowledgment, but that is not my biggest concern in all of this."

"What is?" he asked, pleased by her unwavering response.

"What will Julian think of his maman if he finds out—"

"—he was conceived before we were married?"

"No." Antonia hunched her shoulders and put a finger to her lips. "We will keep that our little secret, yes?"

"Always." The Duke scooped her up to carry her to their bedchamber. "If not that, then what?"

"That his maman behaved no better than a conceited Spartan matriarch, holding him up naked for the inspection and approval of the French king and his court!"

"But you have every right to your conceit, *ma vie*. We have a fine healthy son."

"We do. And that pleases me very much. But surely it will not please *him* when he learns about his first public appearance before royalty?"

"As he is too young to remember the episode, it will pass into folklore soon enough, and you can decide to give it validity or not. Whereas my first appearance before a king I will never forget."

"Oh? Please tell me!"

The Duke carried her from the room. "Perhaps in the morning," he teased. "You're tired."

"How can I sleep from wondering!"

He looked down at her from under heavy lids and said airily, "You will sleep better if I wait—"

"No. And you know it. Tell me."

"Even if it may give you a sleepless night?"

"But why would it do that? You are teasing me!"

"Remember that I did warn you."

"I will," she stated and settled back in his arms, head on his shoulder as he carried her to their bedchamber. "Now please, begin your bedtime story."

"A bedtime story? Very well... I was five years old when presented to the Sun King," he told her, looking down the length of the *enfilade* to where two liveried footmen stood to attention by a set of inlaid double doors, but in his mind's eye recalling that day many years ago. "In the days leading up to my—er—presentation, my mother was at pains to press upon me what a great honor I was being done. That I must make the king my very best bow."

"I do not doubt that you practised to make this bow over and over."

"I did. I remember being well pleased with myself. What a pity the story does not have a happy ending."

"No?" Antonia was intrigued.

He gently set her down on the deep carpet just inside their bedchamber. A fire crackled in the grate, and the gold leaf on wallpaper and furnishings glowed, everything bathed in soft candlelight. He continued with his recollection.

"My parents lived in the age when Louis dazzled all before him. And they expected me to be dazzled also. After all, he was the Sun King, master of all, his majesty ordained by God... But I was not—er—*dazzled*. Why do you think that was?"

Antonia was unequivocal. "You were five. Not much more than an infant." And taking his hand, she led him to the tall canopied bed with its silk hangings. "It surprises me your parents they did not foresee the outcome of this auspicious meeting between their five-year-old son and the king of the sun!"

He lifted her to sit upon the silk coverlet, keeping his hands either side of her thighs. "What do you think happened? Indulge me."

She looked at him from under her lashes with a wicked little smile. "Always."

He grinned and dipped to kiss her mouth. "Vixen… Let us indulge each other… But first you tell me how this bedtime story ends."

"Very well."

She slithered across the silk coverlet to lean her shoulders on the bank of pillows against the padded headboard. He followed her up onto the bed and lay on the mattress before her, propped up on an elbow, gaze never leaving her face. In her mind's eye, Antonia saw the meeting of proud parents and their son and heir, with Louis the Fourteenth. Dressed in their best silks, within the majestic marble and gilt surroundings of the Versailles palace, the couple bowed and curtseyed before the most illustrious and cele-brated monarch in all the world.

"You were a little boy with your head filled with expectations of meeting a wondrous being. But while your parents believed this to be so, and this is how everyone at Court saw the Sun King, *you* saw something else entirely, yes?"

The Duke gently wiggled her stockinged toe. "And what did my five-year-old self see, *ma chérie?*"

"The Sun King, he was how old at the time—?"

"Seventy-four."

"Then you saw not a Sun King, but an old man absurdly dressed in velvet and silks, in a big wig of curled woman's hair, and wearing high red heels. And when *Sa Majesté* opened his mouth —? *Ça alors!*" Her eyes widened. "I think perhaps that not one tooth did he have in his head, yes?" She pulled a face. "Such a vision, it is not a little boy's idea of splendid majesty is it?" Adding in awed exaggeration, playing to her audience of one, "The King to you was one of the Oneiroi! A nightmare come to life! Morpheus in human form. But as you were yet to learn your Greek tales, *Sa Majesté* presented as perhaps a macabre circus performer on his last leg. But the King's legs in their red heels were possibly the only part of him which remained shapely until the end, because the rest of him it was rotting from the inside out!"

When the Duke fell back on the mattress laughing, Antonia scrambled over to kneel beside him.

"You are laughing at me for describing the great Sun King's shapely legs and toothless smile," she lovingly chastised, long hair framing her face. "But what are those legs to you, a terrified little boy, when the rest of him was such a decaying mess?"

"I am not laughing at you, *ma vie*, but at your description of *Sa Majesté*. And yes, his—er—legs! You are right. My five-year-old self cared little for the muscle in his calves. I saw him as you precisely described—a toothless circus performer with too much hair!"

Antonia's eyes lit up with anticipation. "You screamed?"

"I did. And kicked the royal shin through my skirts."

She drew in a breath. "*Parbleu non*! And your parents they were mortified I do not doubt it."

"Beyond words. We never returned here—"

"—to the palace?"

"To this villa."

Antonia's eyes went very round and she sat back on her haunches. She was astounded. "*This* was your parents' villa?"

The Duke propped up on an elbow again. "That shocks you more than my five-year-old self kicking the Sun King's shapely leg?"

"Why of course! You let me choose where we were to live and I chose your parents' house? How is that possible?"

He played with a long strand of her honey curls, wrapping it about a finger, and said pensively, "For the sake of correctness, this wing was once my parents' villa. I purchased the villa beside it many years ago, and turned both into one house—"

"—with a view to making it a home?"

"To be utterly truthful, I'm not certain I had any particular—er—view at that time, *mignonne*. I just wished to preserve the house that held so many happy memories for my parents and, I suspect, for me when I was still in skirts."

She asked shyly, "What if—what if I had chosen one of the other houses you showed me, and not this one?"

"Then we would have made that house our home."

"Thank you for letting me choose."

"Thank you for choosing this villa. But it would not have mattered had you chosen elsewhere," he added gently, "because my home is wherever you are, *ma vie*."

Overcome with emotion, Antonia's throat constricted and her eyes filled with tears. All she could do was nod. She lay down beside him and snuggled in. They lay silent and still, happy in each other's arms, she saying with a sigh of contentment, "Monseigneur, this, too, is fate playing a hand."

"Is that so?"

"It is. I believe it. You must, too."

He rested his chin lightly on the top of her head. "I am beginning to suspect you and the Moirai are co-conspirators."

Antonia giggled. "Oh I hope so! But I have warned them to stay away from our bedchamber. M'sieur le Duc's singular attentions belong to me, and mine to him. We are bound forevermore."

At that pronouncement, he tumbled with her on the bed until she was under him, he taking his weight on his forearms. Looking down at the mischievous twinkle in her green eyes and the accompanying cheeky smile, he grinned, then murmured, before kissing her passionately, "M'sieur le Duc wouldn't have it any other way…"

THIRTEEN

Lord Vallentine spent a congenial hour in fencing practice with the Duke, without a thought about the events of the previous day. The winter sky had not a cloud. The sun shone brightly. The air was crisp and cool. The deserted courtyard had been swept and sawdust strewn about to ensure there were no slipping hazards. And while both noblemen were weary—the Duke spending yesterday on the King's hunt, and Vallentine giving a fencing exhibition at *La Grande Écurie*—it did not dull their competitiveness or determination to best the other, if not in physical endurance then in skill and placement.

Finally, both conceding they were well matched in this bout, they put aside their swords to take refreshment, billowy white shirts damp, natural hair ruffled, a light dust covering the polished sheen of their black leather jockey boots. Footmen offered tumblers of light ale, which were quickly dispatched, Lord Vallentine smacking his lips with satisfaction and sticking out his empty tumbler for a second pour.

They were leaning against a half wall which divided the courtyard from the vegetable garden, tired but relaxed, so relaxed that

Vallentine allowed himself a moment of hubris. As always, when alone, the two best friends spoke in English. Which meant the servants attending them hadn't a clue as to the content of their conversation.

"I might not be as agile as I once was, but there's nothin' wrong with what's up here," he declared, a stab at his temple, "for quick-thinkin' my way into an *attaque au fer*! And so I showed those presumptuous pups who thought they could *balestra* and *beat* me into an *esquive*! Ha!"

"Another day passes with you maintaining your moniker of greatest swordsman in all France and England. I congratulate you, Lucian. I do not doubt the pupils of *La Grande Écurie* did also."

"To a man. They had to concede I'm not a pushover—yet!"

"Bravo. Not a pushover in swordplay, but in your—er—good offices mayhap?"

Lord Vallentine was puzzled. "I did offer pointers to a group of the most promisin' young men, and all were keen to learn, and none appeared to take my advice for granted…" He frowned into his friend's dark eyes. "What d'you mean precisely?"

"You found my—or should I say Montbelliard's—visiting card on your pillow last night or you would not have been here promptly at eight this morning."

Mention of the Chevalier Montbelliard had Vallentine huffing with guilty laughter. He tried to brush aside the young man's visit.

"Oh *that*. Never more surprised of anythin' in all my days than when the lad turned up at your door. Damme! Talk about presumption! To think he presented his card thinkin' he'd be welcomed with open arms as one of the family!"

"And was he?"

"Was he what?"

"Welcomed."

"Not by me!" Vallentine snapped and quickly added when the Duke raised a quizzical eyebrow, "That don't mean to say I was bad-mannered. But I didn't welcome him with open arms either.

And before you ask it, I was the only one in your house to make his acquaintance."

"With coffee and macarons. What a congenial and—er—forward-thinking host."

"Eh?"

"You were surprised by Montbelliard's visit. You didn't welcome him. But no sooner had the surprise visitor put a shoe into my foyer than he was offered coffee and macarons. Of which you both partook."

"He didn't stay above ten minutes," Vallentine stated, ignoring the incongruities in his explanation. "And I got him out of here *subito*! Well, as soon as he'd downed one cup of coffee, yes. But I thought the best way to have him leave was to agree to accompany him to *La Grande Écurie*. Which was where I was headin' anyway, so having him along for company was not an imposition." He frowned. "But I made him no promises!"

"If promises were made, it was well and truly before he sat down to share coffee and cake with you."

"Eh?"

The Duke took a deep breath. He could see his friend was genuinely puzzled so he stirred himself to ask, "How is it that Montbelliard was of the misguided belief he was welcome to present his visiting card at *my* door, the sworn enemy of his nearest relative?"

Lord Vallentine shrugged and was honest. "I would hazard a guess that has somethin' to do with the fact he was one of a number of your Salvan relatives who attended a soiree in my dear wife's—your dearest sister's—salon. As I recall, he came in the carriage of one of the ancient aunts... Now which one was it? Ah yes! Mme de Chavigny—*Tante Victoire*. She brought the lad along, and he left with her, too. He was introduced to me as Cousin Hugh, with no family name mentioned—"

"Cunning lot, the ancient aunts. But they have their uses." The Duke was thinking of Antonia's upcoming presentation at Court.

He had pressed his *Tante Victoire* into coming out of her retirement and returning to Court for the specific purpose of being his wife's sponsor. Still, he could not help sighing his annoyance. "Not that the boy's family name of Montbelliard would have registered with you, so I don't know why my Salvan aunts felt the need to bother trying to cloak his family association. I interrupted. You were saying…?"

Lord Vallentine shrugged. "There ain't much else to add. But you're right. I had no idea who the lad was, or his connection to the Salvans, other than he was of that family. But you have so many relatives on the French side, that he was just another number. Though that didn't stop me noticin' he don't look much like a Salvan—"

"—because his mother was from Guadeloupe, granddaughter of a plantation owner and a freed slave?"

"I did not know that, but aye, that would explain it. And you could've slapped me with a wet fish to find out the lad was Salvan's great-nephew and now his heir! But it don't surprise me you know, even though you've never met him."

When the Duke made no immediate comment, Lord Vallentine filled the silence by signalling for his frockcoat. He was suddenly cold, no longer warm from the exercise. The footmen brought both coats, and helped shrug the noblemen back into them. The Duke tugged on the cuffs of his white shirt and said with bitter certainty,

"My French relatives are deluded if they presume for one moment I will forget or forgive the events that transpired at Treat earlier this year."

"You shouldn't! I wouldn't!"

"And yet," the Duke added silkily, "it would seem they have done so by taking to their bosom the Chevalier Montbelliard?"

Lord Vallentine was sheepish. "Some would argue that just because the lad is next in line to inherit Salvan's accursed title it don't mean he is anythin' like him. And from my observations of him, he seems as far from that evil weasel in temperament and outlook as it is possible to get."

"You were able to scrutinize his—er—character and his motives after observing him upon three occasions: In Estée's drawing room, yesterday at my villa over coffee and macarons. Ah! And your visit to *La Grande Écurie*. I applaud your perspicacity, my dear Lucian."

Lord Vallentine's awkwardness increased. "When you put it like that, it's not much to go on, is it? You think there's more to the lad than meets the eye?"

The Duke produced his gold and enamel snuffbox and tapped the lid with one long finger, a sidelong look at his best friend. "He may very well be as he presents. I am yet to discover all there is to know about Hubert Gabriel Louis Hyacinth Salvan Montbelliard. But I will. And when I do, I will make a determination of where to place him within the family fold, or leave him out of it. For the time being I cannot discount that he may well be a marionette, and his strings being pulled by my repellent cousin. Or for that matter, any number of—er—persons who would like their revenge on me for this, that and—er—the other."

"Ha! Most particularly the other!" Lord Vallentine said with a laugh. "There are possibly too many *persons* to count, with broken hearts and affronted husbands, who'd like their revenge on you, and use any means at their disposal to have it!"

"Such as use Montbelliard for their purposes? Credulous or not. Yes," drawled the Duke, unruffled by Lord Vallentine's assertions. "Perhaps you are right. Be assured that I will look farther afield than my Salvan relatives, or the man himself to ensure I have an accurate assessment of *Cousin Hugh*." He flicked open the lid of the snuffbox and offered Vallentine a pinch of powder and took snuff. "He tried to present his card to the Duchess?"

"Aye. He did. But she was polite and sent her excuses."

The Duke's features softened and he smiled. "She would. She is wise."

"She'd never do anythin' that was counter to your wishes or your welfare. But you know that."

"I do."

"If you want my opinion—"

"Always."

"It's not only your Salvan relatives and the broken hearts who deserve your scrutiny. I'd be lookin' across the Channel at the other branch of your family tree for a culprit amongst your English cousins who wishes you more harm than good, and who may be pullin' strings! And one brimmin' with jealous spite."

The Duke smiled crookedly. "You're referring to Antonia's grandmother Augusta."

"I am. And I wouldn't be tellin' tales beyond the clubroom gaming table if I said that viper has a spy in your household."

"I suspected…" the Duke ruminated. He looked at Vallentine directly. "Antonia told you she believes that to be the case?"

"She did. She don't know who yet, but she is convinced it's a female."

Roxton frowned and spoke his thoughts aloud. "I wonder why she did not mention—"

"She doesn't wish to burden you with it. Says you have enough on your plate…" It was Vallentine's turn to frown. "And that is sharing a confidence I'd prefer you kept to yourself, because she'd not be happy I told you." He sighed. "But there are any number of ways you could've found that out for yourself, so I don't feel as if I've breached *her* confidence." When the Duke remained silent, he added lightly, "So what is it you want me to do about Montbelliard?"

"Do? My dear Lucian, nothing—yet. You are free to give him as many lessons in footwork and foil placement as you please, in the public space of *La Grande Écurie*. And I encourage you to do so—"

"So I can report back on the lad?"

"Give me your honest—er—appraisal, yes. And he may, in

time, confide in you. Whereas he would be disinclined to do so with the ancient aunts, or Estée. I want to know why he is so keen to make Antonia's acquaintance. And until I know one way or the other if Salvan, or anyone else, has any part in Montbelliard's motivations, he won't be welcome here or at the hotel. Nor will I allow him to approach the Duchess for any reason. I need to know my wife and son are safe at all times." He smiled thinly. "Estée will have to forgo the pleasure of that particular cousin's company in her drawing room, or anywhere else within the hotel. I will let you relay that edict to her—"

"Consider it done!"

The Duke inclined his head. "I appreciate you relieving me of what would have been an—er—irksome interview with my sister. Oh, and know that if she continues to correspond with Montbelliard, I will continue to intercept and read those letters."

Vallentine was untroubled by this unabashed breach to his wife's privacy. In fact, he gave his wholehearted support for the Duke's underhanded methods by offering him another piece of advice. "If you want to know what Salvan's up to, I'd be interceptin' the Lady Strathsay's correspondence with the Duchess. That woman has a knack for unsettlin' the chit with her poisonous patter covered in silky sincerities!"

"How poetic," the Duke quipped, signalling to the footmen they were dismissed. "I agree with you. But I won't ask how you know…" He held His Lordship's gaze with an unblinking stare. "What I do want you to know is that I have never intercepted your correspondence, or read it. Your secrets are safe with you." He smiled thinly. "God forbid I should be accused of no standards whatsoever!"

Lord Vallentine shook his head with a grin.

"You didn't have to say so, but thank you. Not that I have anythin' in m'letters worth your interest. And I certainly don't have any secrets! Ha! If I did, I would tell you. You know that, too, don't you?"

"I do." It was the Duke's turn to let out a small breath and confess further, "Nor do I intercept or read my wife's correspondence. She, too, would tell me if there were anything worth the telling—"

"Of course she would! She only has your best interests at heart, as I told you earlier."

This made the Duke chuckle. It was not a pleasant laugh.

"The heart! Therein lies the chink in my armor! My—er—Achilles heel, if you will. One I never thought to experience. The fates conspired to affect a different outcome. But so be it." He cleared his throat and said levelly, "As a husband I will never take it upon myself to read my wife's letters without her permission. A marriage must have trust as well as love if it is to thrive. And yet, as duke, I confidently predict that there are certain particulars in her correspondence that she is keeping from me, not because she has secrets, but because she sincerely believes, as you say, that she *has my best interests at heart*."

"She would never intentionally—"

"I know that!" Roxton cut in with suppressed emotion. "I also know that with time she will eventually be entirely open with me; that she will come to realise there are occasions where keeping me in ignorance because she wishes to shield me from some unpleasantness can do more harm than good. I must be patient. And I am only confiding this in you because I know she will co-opt you to her cause to—er—protect me, if she hasn't already. Which puts you in the unenviable position of finding a way to keep your word to *her*, without being disloyal to *me*. As you are already adept at the practice with your wife, I do not foresee a problem, do you?"

Lord Vallentine swallowed and slowly shook his head. But even that action made him feel the traitor when he thought about his promise to Antonia not to tell the Duke about Salvan's letter, a letter he was certain had some fundamental underlying message that was vital to his best friend's happiness and peace of mind. A pity Antonia had burned it, and yet, he was glad she had. He wasn't in an unenviable position. He was in an impossible one!

His face portrayed his inner turmoil because the Duke clapped him on the back to wake him from his trance and said in an altogether different voice, as he headed toward the cloister, Vallentine unconsciously following, "Breakfast awaits. You must be starving. Even I find I have an appetite this morning…"

On the terrace, Lord Vallentine waylaid the Duke from going indoors with a hand to his sleeve. He'd had an idea how best to solve his immediate dilemma.

"D'you think the chit's grandmother keeps copies of all her correspondence? Would she, for argument's sake, have an important letter she had been requested to forward to a correspondent, copied out first? So she, too, had a copy of it."

"I know for a fact she had the wax seals carefully removed and then reapplied on the correspondence Antonia wrote me while I remained in Paris and she was in London. Augusta had every one of those letters meticulously copied out." The Duke smiled bitterly. "No matter she withheld the originals from me! But I have those copies now, too."

"I don't doubt it! Nothin' gets past you! And I'm glad to hear it." Lord Vallentine let drop his hand, but his blue eyes remained on his friend's face. "May I suggest that however you discovered that viper's methods for getting her talons on Antonia's correspondence, you apply the same stratagem to discover what other letters she had copied which concern the Duchess." He blinked, adding with a huff of annoyance. "But this time, as I said, she ain't keepin' this correspondence in her top drawer—if you know what I'm gettin' at—"

"Augusta is acting as go-between and sending on letters to the Duchess?"

"I didn't say that. You did."

The Duke's dark brows lifted slowly. "You did. And thank you."

His Lordship gave a snort as he followed his best friend into the warmth of the villa and through to the breakfast room. "No need to thank me! I'm bein' selfish. I want to lay my head on my pillow at night and do what I do every night—Sleep knowin' I've done right by you, and her. And as it so happens, I do sleep like a baby—What the—!" His Lordship swirled about and had his cleft chin pointing skyward to the plaster ceiling at the sudden inexplicable rumble of footfall that proceeded a cacophony of wailing. "Good grief! What—What's goin' on up there?"

Unruffled and unsurprised, the Duke went to the sideboard and calmly poured himself out a dish of coffee. "That, my dear Lucian, is a foretaste of your future. Whoever coined the misnomer *dormir comme un bébé* should be strung up!"

FOURTEEN

AFTER BREAKFAST, Antonia was spending most of the day with her Parisian mantua-makers, and their small army of assistants, being fitted for her Court gown. They arrived with bolts of black velvet (for the Court was still in mourning for the Dauphine), white silk taffetas, and sheer linens, rolls of satin ribbons, and exquisitely fine lace. Armed with tape measures, scissors, and chalk, and hundreds of straight pins, they set to draping, pinning, sewing, and cutting the luxurious materials to fit exactly their noble client's stays and over the wide panniers demanded of Court gowns.

With his duchess suitably occupied, the Duke was able to put into action the plans he had already made with his housekeeper for Antonia's birthday celebration, which was the following day.

The small salon off the main dining room was decorated with an abundance of colorful hothouse blooms in Chinoiserie tubs, and in porcelain pots on ornate pedestals. And so too the adjoining dining room. And when one of the Duchess's birthday gifts arrived from Paris in a tall wooden crate, the housekeeper assured her noble employer that every effort would be made to conceal it. The gift would be unpacked and placed in a corner of the dining room, covered with a sheet, screens put around it, and one or two of the floral arrangements placed in front of the screens. In this way, if the Duchess should happen to wander into the room before her birthday, the flowers would be enough of a distraction and she none the wiser as to the elaborately concealed gift.

In the dining room, the Duke's chandler and his assistants had lowered the chandelier and were busy polishing the crystal and fitting fresh Trudon white beeswax candles, while from the long mahogany table, two leaves had been removed so that it now sat four persons in comfortable proximity. The table was still large enough to hold a delicate silver epergne centrepiece, and several Sevres porcelain baskets filled with an array of colourful pastillage floral arrangements created by the Duke's confectioner. And at each place were the requisite silver, crystal, and porcelain necessary for a sumptuous dining experience.

While these preparations continued under the expert eye of the under-butler, the Duke sauntered about, twirling his quizzing glass by its silken cord, listening to his housekeeper, an eye to the steady stream of footmen and maids who came and went. Satisfied the arrangements met his expectations, he made only one further request—his son's ornate cradle on its pedestal be placed by the Duchess's chair to allow his little lordship to join the celebration.

The Duke then retired to the library where he found Lord Vallentine sprawled out, reading the English newssheets. Their solitude lasted but an hour, when it was disturbed by a footman, who had been instructed by the butler to inform their master when the carriage had returned from Paris.

The footman did so, and when asked, told his master that from the large conveyance a full complement of occupants alighted under the *porte-cochère*: M'sieur le Duc's valet, M'sieur le Duc's head under-valet, and M'sieur le Duc's Parisian tailor with two of his assistants. Following up behind the carriage was a horse and cart carrying a dozen bolts of various fabrics required by M'sieur le Duc's tailor, as well as the travelers' portmanteaux, and two liveried footmen unlike any footmen this footman had ever seen before.

When Lord Vallentine told him to explain himself, the servant gave a nervous snort and his eyes widened, as if he feared being disbelieved. He said that the two men were the size of caged circus bears, and looked just as ferocious, and had arrived to be of service to whatever was in the large wooden crate that had arrived earlier and was now under covers in the dining room.

Lord Vallentine was about ask for further explanation when the Duke waved the footman away without registering surprise or making comment to anything he had been told. He then put aside his newssheet and stood, apologizing to Lord Vallentine for inconveniencing him. His Lordship was required to vacate the library because the Duke needed to have a pressing conversation with his valet. Vallentine unfolded his long legs from the wingchair and graciously took himself off without further ado, privately wondering what it was the valet had done to deserve being called to the library. He was just glad he wasn't the one getting the reprimand—the conversation about the Chevalier Montbelliard had been awkward enough—and he was all sympathy for Ellicott.

Alone, the Duke called for coffee. While he awaited the arrival of his valet, he spent his time reading and replying to the stack of correspondence accumulating on his desk.

MARTIN ELLICOTT ENTERED the library an hour after his return to the villa from the Duke's Parisian mansion, looking less crumpled than when he had alighted the carriage under the *porte-cochère*. He had felt the need to change his clothing, to splash cold water on his face, and to tidy his hair. Cooped up in a carriage with four others had drained him. Not that he was in the habit of making idle conversation with anyone, least of all other servants and merchants. And he certainly didn't offer these men any explanation as to why the Duke had requested they accompany him to the villa, because quite simply, he had no idea.

He had put his complete ignorance to the back of his mind whilst he was busy at the hotel. But now, as he came quietly across the deep carpet carrying the red leather *portefeuille* he had been sent to fetch, he felt a frisson of fretfulness. The hairs at his nape tingled. He could not remember the last time he had ever been summoned to the public rooms used by the Duke's family and his guests, in any of his houses. This was a first, and being out of his milieu troubled him deeply.

And when the Duke kept on with his letter-writing without looking up and merely raised his free hand to point to a group of chairs, not across from the desk, but by the fireplace, the valet did not know if he should leave the *portefeuille* on the desk, or take it with him. Several seconds of indecision and he decided to hold onto it. And there he stood, straight-backed and silent, chin parallel with the carpet, and stared into the flames, not a look about him, at the Duke at his desk, or at any of the floor-to-ceiling bookcases, or the view of the tree-lined avenue beyond the French doors.

As he was used to waiting, to being silent and watchful, and only speaking when spoken to, it never occurred to him to sit. He noticed that on a table central to this collection of furniture was a tray that had upon it a porcelain coffee service and beside it a heavy silver coffee urn on its pedestal. But he also noticed that there was an absence of servants. The footman who had opened the door for him had remained out in the hall. And while the butler was obviously needed elsewhere, there was always an under-butler or upper footman present to cater to his master's needs. Martin Ellicott surmised that the restricted number of servants was because the Duke and Duchess were presently residing at this villa, and there simply wasn't the room to accommodate the usual army of domestics that inhabited the hotel, and in England, the country estate of Treat.

And as he stood silent and waiting, his present predicament hit him like a sickening blow to the chest. He was alone with the Duke. He felt foolish and embarrassed for his reaction to this novel experience, because in his capacity as valet, he had spent almost the past two decades often alone and in close proximity with his noble employer in the privacy of his dressing closet, and in any of the rooms of his private apartments. There his skills and expertise were required and appreciated. But alone with him in a public room was unprecedented and it increased his fretfulness and, ironically for him, was a far more personal and intimate space than any of the private rooms which were part of his domain as the closest servant to the master.

How was he to act? What was he to say? *Why was he here?*

And then the Duke spoke, ending his mental musings and increasing his apprehension tenfold.

"Take a seat, Martin… Coffee?"

The valet almost fainted.

⁂

"Sit," the Duke ordered when Martin Ellicott continued to just stand there, blinking at him.

When at his command the man did as he was told, perching precariously on the end of the cushion of the closest wing chair, heels and knees together, back ramrod-straight, gaze respectfully lowered to the floor, and the *portefeuille* on his lap, Roxton mentally sighed. Not because of his valet's actions—he had expected this response, and the question about coffee was blatant teasing—but because he knew this conversation was going to be a difficult one, for both of them.

Which was why he had been putting it off. But he could no longer do so because tomorrow was Antonia's birthday, and he was determined everything about the day would be perfect for her. And if it was to be a success, then it hinged on the outcome of this interview—conversation, part-confessional—he really had no idea what to call it. All he knew for certain was that they had to get through it to reach the desired result, for everyone concerned. But what the valet did not know, but which the Duke and Duchess were very aware, was that from this day forward Martin Ellicott's life would never be the same again.

Having the upper hand in any given situation was the Duke's forte.

It had not been so when as a boy he'd been forcibly taken from his mother to live with his grandfather. The fourth duke was, without argument, a cold-hearted monster whose cruelty broke his spirit. The old man also almost broke his mind—*almost*, had it not been for the boy who risked his own life by stealing into his room under cover of darkness. This boy showed him kindness and befriended him and was his only humane contact with the outside world in that first year locked away in the English countryside—a land and a people who were as foreign to him as likely inhabitants on the moon.

Martin Ellicott was that boy and the Duke knew that without Martin he would have descended into a malaise from which he may never have recovered. He certainly would have lost what scraps of humanity remained of his previous life with his loving parents. For that alone, he owed him a great debt. And there was a greater debt, for it had been Martin who had put himself in harm's way to save Antonia and her unborn child from a madman.

Recalling his ducal grandfather, and those years under his tyrannical rule, unsettled him. And so he had spent his life since the old man's death never thinking about him at all. As for the threat to the lives of Antonia and Julian, that unimaginable horror was still fresh enough that he could barely speak about it. Now he must speak about both, for Martin Ellicott's sake. And selfishly, for his own sake, he hoped it would put his demons finally to rest.

But it was left to his wife to show him how these debts should be repaid.

These were his thoughts as he poured coffee into two dishes, one of which he sugared. This dish he held out to Martin, who looked at it but did not take it because he did not know what to do with it. He had never eaten or had a drop to drink of any beverage in his master's presence.

"Black with one sugar is how you prefer your coffee is it not?" the Duke asked him in English. When his valet could only nod, fingers curled so tight about the *portefeuille* that the whites of his knuckles showed, the Duke set the dish on its saucer on the small table by the man's elbow. "Then you will enjoy it."

He flicked out the skirts of his velvet frockcoat and sat opposite. Glancing over the rim of his coffee dish he wondered if it had been a mistake to take the man out of his milieu so suddenly. He appeared a fish out of water, gasping with uncertainty and doubt. But he knew that if Martin Ellicott were to breathe easy in the rarefied atmosphere inhabited by members and friends of the Roxton family then he had best embrace change and all its consequences as soon as possible.

Still, he could not resist teasing him a little. After all, the man had no idea what lay ahead and still considered himself his valet. And if Martin was queasy with uneasiness by merely being in this library, the Duke could not wait to see how he dealt with what he was about to bestow upon him. Thus he asked him the one question he knew would get his full attention and have him ignore his surroundings.

"You brought George Geraghty with you?" he asked casually, setting his dish on its saucer.

Martin Ellicott's fingers released from the red leather satchel and he sat a little taller, if that were possible. "I did, Your Grace."

"And has Geraghty, in your opinion, proven his worth as your understudy?"

"Yes, Your Grace. He has exceeded my expectations. He will make a fine valet for some exalted personage."

The Duke feigned concern. "But you seem—er—displeased with him?"

"Not at all, Your Grace."

The Duke chuckled. "Ah! I see. Not displeased with *him*, but with *me*, for making *you* bring him here."

"Your Grace, I—"

"All will become clear to you soon. For now you will have to stew a bit longer." The Duke took a sip from his dish, then said with a thin smile, "I am pleased your assessment of Geraghty aligns with my own. He has exceeded my expectations too. Which is a testament to your care and teaching in preparing him for his future as valet to some—er—*exalted personage*."

"I am glad to hear it, Your Grace."

"It is immensely satisfying that, like you, Geraghty does not *fuss*."

"He does not, Your Grace."

"And the others who were your carriage companions—Did they come along without a—er—whimper?"

"Of course. When M'sieur le Duc d'Roxton requires the services of his tailor, he obeys without question."

The Duke smiled. "Naturally. And now not only are you wondering why George Geraghty is here, but you want to ask me why I need my tailor and his assistants when you provided me with a more than adequate wardrobe from my closet at the hotel? That too will become clear in due course. And Madame, did she—er—present you with a bundle of letters?"

"As you predicted she would, Your Grace. Not one but two. And they were thrust at my chest with threats to my person if I did not deliver them as instructed. I took the liberty of putting them in the *portefeuille*."

"What I subject you to, all in the name of domestic harmony!"

The Duke put aside his dish and stuck out his hand for the

satchel. He set this on his knees and opened the flap. "You of course did not take the—er—liberty of casting your eye at what else was in the satchel?" When there was silence, he looked up in time to catch Martin pursing his lips. He smiled crookedly. "Naturally you did not, or you would not be sitting there wondering what is going on and letting your coffee go cold." And with that cryptic comment he took out the two bundles of letters tied up with pink ribbon and dropped them beside his chair at his feet. "I would dearly love to toss them into the grate. But I shall restrain myself... Remind me the day after tomorrow—I won't spoil the Duchess's birthday—that letters have arrived from my sister, and we will both be suitably surprised."

"Yes, Your Grace. I won't forget."

"I know you won't," came the reply, this time said without artifice and accompanied by a rare genuine smile. When this had the valet scrambling for his coffee dish, the Duke chuckled. "Dear me, Martin. Have I always been such a hard taskmaster that a kind word and a smile is enough to unseat you?"

Martin shook his head vigorously. "No-no, Your Grace. It's just —I have no notion as to why I am here, or what you want of me, or what I may have done to-to displease you. Thus I am—I am— *disquieted*."

"I do not doubt it," the Duke replied. He rummaged in the satchel, and satisfied everything was in order, closed the flap and tucked it between the padded chair arm and his thigh. He then sat back with an expression that was hard to read. What he said next not only surprised the valet, but unsettled him further. "Do you recall when I first came to Treat?"

"I beg your pardon, your Grace?"

"You heard correctly. I vowed never to speak about that time but—" He lifted a hand on a sigh. "And yet, here we are. So, do you remember or not?"

"I do, Your Grace. As if it were yesterday."

That did surprise the Duke. "Truly? Why?"

"That I should remember it so particularly?"

"Yes. I thought, like me, you'd find it too disturbing to commit to memory."

Martin Ellicott smiled bashfully. He could not help himself. "May I speak candidly, Your Grace?"

"I would be disappointed if you did not."

"I understand why *you* would want to forget that day—indeed why you would want to forget those years… But for me…? Your arrival at the estate was the most momentous event to have happened in my short life. I was only eight years old. And so it is etched in my memory."

"I am sorry to hear it—"

"I beg your pardon, Your Grace. There is nothing to apologize for. I do not mean it was momentous because it was distressing. It was not—for me."

"I did not know that… Then again, I have never asked you about that day nor that time, have I? That was remiss of me. Will you indulge my curiosity and tell me why it was so—er—momentous for you?"

The valet allowed his gaze to flicker across to meet the Duke's dark eyes. "I had never met anyone like you. Nor have I met anyone to equal you since. I hope that admission does not offend you."

"Not in the least." The Duke huffed. "But that does not explain the earth-shattering nature my arrival seems to have had on you. Unless it was because it was the first time you had ever seen a child who was more wild, wounded animal than boy—untamed, unkempt, and unable to restrain his terror…?" He tried to be indifferent. "No doubt my—er—screaming terror tantrums at the top of my lungs in my native tongue were—er—unforgettable."

Martin Ellicott remained serious, gaze dropping to the diamond-encrusted shoe buckle of his master's right shoe as he recalled that day in his mind's eye.

"I was the only child up at the house. And as I was not permitted to roam beyond the grounds, and children were forbidden from entering the estate, if I did see a child, it was from some distance." He brought his eyes back up to the Duke's face and dared to allow himself a small smile. "So regardless of how you presented upon your arrival, or how frightening you first appeared, I was overjoyed you had come."

The Duke shifted uneasily on his chair. "And yet I did not treat you at all—*well*."

"You treated me precisely as expected—with suspicion. Why would you easily accept kindness from a stranger when your own flesh and blood—your grandfather—treated you despicably?"

There was a moment's silence when all that was heard was the ticking of the mantel clock, and then the Duke spoke, and in a voice Martin had rarely heard; the tightly controlled anguish sent his own throat dry.

"The old duke—my grandfather—was a pitiless, wretched old man capable of—capable of great cruelty… To do what he did to a boy not twelve years of age… I'd not have believed it possible, were I not that boy."

"Your Grace, pardon my frankness, but the old duke treated his horses and his dogs better than he did you!" the valet stated hotly. "In that first year we thought he might succeed in killing you."

This made the Duke shake his head and smile crookedly. His old manner returned.

"Kill me? No. He was determined to make me—er—suffer. But he had no wish for me to die. With my father's untimely death, I became his only heir. Had I died too, it would have been the end of the Roxton dukedom. And the old man had poured too much wealth into that monolith of a house to see it dissipate amongst distant relatives. But he did do his best to beat the French blood out of me when I refused to speak anything but my mother's tongue—"

"How could you speak anything else when you knew no English?"

"Is that what you thought? No. I understood the language. My father spoke to me in English. I was just incalcitrant." He frowned in puzzlement. "But you were French. Or at least your mother was. How did the old duke not know that?"

"It was my mother's parents who were French. My father made her promise to only speak her native tongue in the privacy of our rooms. He knew the old duke's hatred of all things French was because His Lordship your father remained in Paris and refused to return to England. And so we concealed our French connections."

"And yet you risked being discovered, not only by sneaking into my locked room via the priest hole, but by conversing with me in French. That was brave of you, and of your parents. Had you been discovered I do not doubt the old man would've tossed all three of you out into the wilderness, and without the requisite reference to gain future employment."

Martin Ellicott smiled. "If I had known you understood English, I may have kept my French linguistic skills hidden from you too. But I did not. I thought that if I spoke your native tongue you would know me for friend rather than foe."

The Duke brushed an imaginary fleck of lint from his velvet knee and said, the rasp back in his voice, "I remember—I remember you tried your best to befriend me, and to—to console me... I was a most ungrateful sullen wretch. I preferred my misery."

"Your father had only recently died and you'd been torn away from your mother. And your grandfather locked you up and never showed you one ounce of compassion. Your grief and fear were understandable."

"What I do remember most particularly is your insistence that I pretend to fall in with my grandfather's demands. That if I were to act as if upon a stage, my life would take a turn for the better."

"I was repeating what my parents had told me to advise you. I did not precisely comprehend what they meant."

"I scoffed at your suggestion. I, a Salvan by blood, son of the Marquis of Alston, was to lower myself to that of a—er—common actor—men who earn their living by lying? Even then, as a stripling and in my grief, I was so damnably arrogant! But I also remember what you said that finally made me receptive to your suggestion."

"Which was?"

"That the old duke was undeserving of knowing my true feelings and thoughts. That I should tell him what he wanted to hear and nothing more."

"Again, that was my parents' advice. My mother made me repeat it several times so that I was assured of telling you word-for-word what she had told me."

"Your mother was a wise woman. That was the turning point for me."

"To becoming an actor, Your Grace?"

"A very good actor, Martin. Concealing my thoughts and feelings from the world became a way of life, a way of surviving the wretchedness of my existence. I was so good at it that with time I hardly knew when not to act. And I have, in part, been—er—acting ever since." The Duke smiled at some private thought. "The Duchess tells me I have done such a marvellous job of hiding behind a façade that I've managed to conceal my feelings from myself! She is quite right." He lost his smile and held Martin Ellicott's gaze. "I have never expressed my gratitude to you, or to your parents, for-for—for what you did to ease my-my —loneliness and-and my suffering that first year I came to England."

"Perhaps not in words, Your Grace. But you have done so by your actions."

"How so?"

"You do not recall the promise you made me several months

into your incarceration, a promise to one day make me your valet?"

"While I was still locked up? I had presumed that promise was made much later, before I went off to Oxford with Lord Vallentine."

"Upon your return from your university studies was when I became your valet, that is true. But the promise you made was much earlier."

"I should like to hear how this promise came about."

Martin Ellicott made the Duke a quaint little bow of the head in acquiescence.

"It was at the end of your first six months at the estate, and for your good behavior at finally only speaking in English with your minders, you were permitted warm water and fresh linens. It was your final night in your old room. The next day you were being moved to your own apartment on the other side of the house. Which meant no more visits from me via the priest hole. We had a special supper prepared by my mother. And at its conclusion you made a formal speech..."

The valet grinned and shook his head at the memory, and then continued, a glance across at the Duke who was all rapt attention.

"You said that for my services to the Marquis d'Alston, which you told me was you—although I already knew this because everyone had been ordered to call you Alston—and for my wise counsel, you declared that when you became M'sieur le Duc d'Roxton—that is how you styled yourself even then—you would anoint me your valet—"

"*Anoint*? Surely I meant appoint?"

"You did. But no matter to me. Anoint or appoint, I was suitably awed. Particularly as you made this declaration—if you can believe me, but it is true—standing atop a foot stool, and me kneeling with head bowed before you, a broom handle substituting for your sword placed upon my shoulder—"

The Duke burst out laughing. "Did I, by God! What supercilious bravado for a filthy little wretch with matted hair and wearing tatters! I believe it of me, so I believe you. I only wish I had a memory of it."

Martin was unabashed. "The entire ceremony obviously made a deeper impression on me than it did you, Your Grace. Particularly the part where you assured me that even when you escaped from Treat you would return one day to rescue me—"

"—like a knight of old!? Was I returning with an army of devoted followers at my back?"

"You were good to your word. You did return, not with an army but one devoted follower—Lord Vallentine. And you did make me your valet. Me, the son of a housekeeper and a butler, who had only ever been an under-footman."

"I made you my personal servant, Martin. That is hardly rescuing you."

"Pardon, Your Grace. But it was a rescue as far as I was concerned. I was made valet to a duke, and not just any duke but the premier duke in England. That is a great honor. And I have wanted for nothing ever since. With you I have travelled all over Europe, to the Levant, and beyond. I have your trust, and that, too, is an honor, for you do not trust many. I have led a charmed life. Not one day would I alter. Not a single one. It has been a privilege and a pleasure to not only serve you, Your Grace, but to know you."

"I hardly deserve your devotion, Martin," the Duke replied with an embarrassed huff at being so openly venerated. "But it pleases me you have no regrets. Though that makes what I am about to impose upon you that much more difficult to enact." He sighed, uncrossed his legs and drew the *portefeuille* back across his lap. "I should have done this a long time ago. Truth told—and you know this better than anyone—I am a selfish creature, and one of habit. I cannot imagine anyone taking your place. But our world, such as we knew it, was upended a twelvemonth ago almost to the day, was it not? And our lives have not been the same since." He permitted himself to smile softly. "I would not have it any other way. I am confident you feel the same as—"

"Wholeheartedly, Your Grace!" Martin interrupted enthusiastically, and unconsciously let out a sigh of contentment. "The Duchess has brought sunshine into all our lives, and his little lordship has brought out the stars."

"Just so," murmured the Duke, not at all surprised by his valet's over-joyous response, and strangely affected by it. So much so that he took a moment to collect himself, rummaging in the satchel and extracting several papers, which he placed on top of the *portefeuille*, before saying levelly, "The Duchess had only one wish for her birthday. And I am determined it will be granted, today."

He put his hand flat on the papers and looked across at his valet who was still smiling. He knew his next words would wipe that smile away, but they had to be said.

"Martin, the time has come for you to step aside as my valet."

FIFTEEN

MARTIN ELLICOTT'S smile dissolved, and his face drained of color. He swallowed and struggled to remain calm.

"George Geraghty—Geraghty is here to replace me!?"

"As my valet? Yes. But—"

Martin Ellicott shot to his feet. "I understand." He formally bowed his head, then steeled himself to look the Duke in the face. "You need not say another word, Your Grace. I—"

"You do not under—"

"—will treasure my years with you—"

"You wish to leave me?"

"Wh—no! Yes! If that is what you want—"

"Why would I want that?"

Martin Ellicott frowned. "But—Your Grace! You have replaced me with George Geraghty."

"I have. But that does not answer the question of why you would want to leave."

"I must! I cannot stay!"

"Why not?"

Martin Ellicott wondered why the Duke was goading him, and beyond what was tolerable. One minute they were reminiscing about shared boyhood experiences, and in the next breath he was told he was being replaced as valet. And now he was being asked why he would want to leave his employment. Which was the last thing he would ever have dreamed of doing. He felt all at sea.

"Please allow me to leave with some dignity intact—"

"But I don't want you to leave, Martin. With or without your dignity."

"You don't? I-I do not understand. I thought it must be because I had become an embarrassment."

"Embarrassment?" The Duke was intrigued. He sat back and demanded, "Explain."

The valet swallowed and rubbed his hands together. Realising his palms were damp, he whipped his hands behind his back, and put up his chin.

"You know it is not my practice to take notice or comment on below stairs gossip, unless Your Grace specifically requests it of me. And I have always maintained my distance from the household, as is appropriate for one in my position. I have pressed this upon George Geraghty. And I can assure you, Your Grace, that as well as being a fine valet, Geraghty is an exceptionally circumspect creature, who keeps to himself. You can be confident of his absolute discretion and unequivocal loyalty."

"Coming from you, that is high praise indeed. I would not have appointed him otherwise."

Martin Ellicott's nostrils quivered. "He knows?"

"He does indeed know." The Duke couldn't help a crooked smile. "A small test… And you will be pleased your pupil did not disappoint—"

"—because he did not let on to me you were replacing me with him?"

The Duke inclined his head. "I had to make certain he lived up to my expectations, and—er—yours. But you were telling me about your embarrassment…?"

"I beg your pardon. It is not so much my embarrassment, as yours, Your Grace. There are those amongst the upper servants who disapprove of me having the honor of being his little lordship's godfather."

"How is that an embarrassment for either of us?"

Martin Ellicott couldn't help a wry smile. "I do not know of any other servant on either side of the Channel who has the singular honor of being appointed godfather to a nobleman's son, least of all the heir to a dukedom, do you?"

"What of it? I don't give tuppence for what others think. You know that better than anyone."

"Lord Vallentine as godfather, that is understandable. He is your best friend and your brother-in-law. He is also heir to an earldom and a swordsman par excellence. Whereas I—I am of humble stock, and a-a valet, and I—"

"I believe it was Cicero who said—and I do not own to having it word perfect—that our characters are formed not from the blood of our forefathers, but by circumstances that form our habits, and by which we are nurtured and live." The Duke threw up a hand. "You were born on the estate. Your parents were hardworking and honorable, who led by example. I want my son to learn by example. You have served me with the utmost loyalty for almost twenty years. You saved the lives of my wife and son, putting yourself in harm's way to do so. You are the best of men, Martin. As far as the Duchess and I are concerned, that makes you eminently qualified to be Julian's godfather."

"Thank—thank you, Your Grace," Martin Ellicott murmured, so overcome that his bottom lip quivered and he had to drop his gaze to the carpet because he could not see through the film of sudden tears. He heaved a heavy sigh and tried to make good his escape before he fell all to pieces. "If you—if you will excuse me, Your Grace. I-I must pack—"

"Pack?"

"You will want me to remove my personal effects and vacate my room as soon as possible so that Geraghty can—"

"That is unimportant. What is—"

"But I do not want to be in the way when he—"

"Martin. I have told you that I do not want you to leave."

"I am sorry, Your Grace. I must. I cannot stay. I no longer have a position in your household. And at this moment in time I-I need to—I need to-to decide what and where and how I-I—I need to be alone to-to—"

The Duke's jaw set hard. "*Sit.*"

Instantly Martin Ellicott's buttocks were back on the wingchair's cushion. But he could not raise his chin off his chest.

"Why do you instantly assume you must leave? Or that I wish to replace you?" the Duke demanded with an annoyed sigh.

The valet blinked, tears splashing his black woollen breeches, and he quickly dabbed at his eyes with his clean linen handkerchief. "But—but you have replaced me, Your Grace."

The Duke's gaze shot to the ornate plastered ceiling, and he bit back a retort. Taking a deep breath, he told Martin Ellicott to look at him. And when the valet did, the Duke held his glassy-eyed gaze, and said with icy restraint, "Do not imagine this interview is any easier for me… As I told you earlier, I have been putting this off for months. But here we are. And the course for our future has already been set. So the time for argument is long past. We now must get on with it so we can all return to some semblance of regularity. To be frank, this back and forth banter is fatiguing. Thus, you will give me the courtesy of hearing me out without interruption. When I am finished, you will have the opportunity to speak as freely as you wish, and without apology. After all, you are no longer my valet, but a—er—free agent…"

When the Duke paused, awaiting Martin Ellicott's assent, the valet did not know whether he had permission to speak or not. He kept his lips pressed together and nodded vigorously.

"From today, Geraghty takes on the position of valet," the Duke stated. "It is a small—er—bump in the domestic harmony of my houses, and one that I have been assured by Geraghty will cause minimal disruption for all concerned, principally me." The Duke smiled crookedly. "Given the monumental upheavals I have already experienced in the past twelve months this is as nothing. But for you…? Your life, Martin, is about to be turned upside down. Be assured—while you may have been replaced as my valet, *you* cannot be replaced. The Duchess tells me you are *irreplaceable*. I agree with her."

Martin Ellicott's eyes widened and his mandible dropped.

"Good. Speechless *and* ears wide open!" the Duke quipped. "I need not then repeat myself. I do not doubt that what I am about to tell you will take some time for you to fully digest. These are copies of documents held with my attorneys, and signed by me," he added, long fingers to the papers atop the leather satchel. "They are for you, and to read later at your leisure. Set out in them are the provisions of your settlement—for want of a better term. There are no—er—conditions attached. All that is required of you in return is to graciously accept this new life, and—dare I need tell you—enjoy it." He smiled thinly. "Why, I am sure you are asking yourself, am I bestowing this upon you at this particular time? Simply? Because tomorrow is the Duchess's birthday, and this new life you are about to embark upon is the only gift she asked of me.

"Therefore it behoves me to advise you in the strongest possible language to accept your new life, if you do not want to disappoint *her*." The Duke grinned and shook his head at a memory before coughing into his fist and continuing. "The Duchess held up the metaphorical looking glass and had me peer into it to see what was self-evident. That since the age of twelve, you have been the one constant in my life, the person whom I could trust above all others. She quoted Montaigne's words that few men are admired by their servants. Yet the fact that I am still held in high esteem by *you*, a man of principle and valour who has been my valet for almost half my life, she said, was an honor done *me*… Tenacious and ever truthful, Martin. That is the Duchess." He huffed good-naturedly. "And we are all the better for it, are we not? So let me tell you what is in these documents—Ah! But first perhaps another dish of coffee would help revive your color…?"

Martin Ellicott shot up off the wingchair with the intention of pouring the coffee for the Duke, but he was so light-headed he almost pitched forward. He grabbed quickly for the chair back and closing his eyes took a deep breath. By the time he was able to stand tall, the Duke was at the silver urn pouring out into two clean dishes.

The Duke placed one dish on its saucer on the table by Martin Ellicott's wingchair, and told him to sit and drink up. He sipped his coffee by the urn, an eye on Martin, then returned to his chair. The *portefeuille* and documents he left propped by a chair leg. He knew them almost word-for-word, having gone over each several times with his attorneys, his man of business, and with Antonia. And now it only remained to inform Martin Ellicott.

He waited until Martin had set aside the empty dish, and sat perched on the cushion in his customary manner, fearing that had he spoken while the man was still drinking, he may well have spluttered coffee down the front of his pristine linen waistcoat in the surprise of discovery of just what was being bestowed upon him. The Duke came straight to the point.

"Martin, I have made you a gentleman of independent means. You are to have a thousand a year for life, as well as a clothing allowance, and the use of a small apartment in each of my houses which will accommodate you and your manservant. And when you feel the need for some respite from the family fold, I have put at your disposal Moran Hall. It is a quaint manor house built in the time of Queen Anne, on the outskirts of Bath in Somerset-shire. It has been leased to you for your lifetime at a peppercorn rent. The house is presently being refurbished and new furniture acquired. There are tenants attached to the acreage, and their rents and yields are sufficient for the upkeep of the house, the gardens, and parkland in which it sits. I am told the house has a fine prospect of the hills and woodlands. Any major repairs will be undertaken by my duchy, and my man of business will send a representative twice a year to survey the property.

"There are other particulars about the Hall, as well as the financial settlements regarding the payment of your allowance, but I need not go into those now. Read through these documents and if you find anything amiss, you need only tell me. Ah! And before I forget. While my tailor is here to fit me for a Court mourning ensemble, I have instructed him to measure you for several suits, and a dozen shirts, and whatever else you may require. M'sieur is only too willing to oblige me. Of course none of these superlative sartorial articles will be ready in time for the Duchess's birthday celebration. But I do not doubt you have at least one elegant frockcoat in your wardrobe to wear to dinner."

When Martin Ellicott stared across at the Duke as if in a stupor, unable to speak, unable to move, unable to fully comprehend what was being bestowed upon him, the Duke smiled in understanding.

"It is a great deal to take in, is it not? No doubt you will need to—er—sleep on it. And lest you think your changed circumstances something conjured up in a befuddled dream, I suggest you have these documents close at hand. And be assured, whatever you decide to do with the rest of your life as a gentleman of independent means—remain as part of my family or walk out of here to pursue a life elsewhere—you will always be welcome to return, and to visit. And if you do leave us, I would expect at the very least a regular correspondence. Antonia would never forgive you if you did not send the odd letter asking after your godson. But that is entirely up to y—"

"Stay!" Martin blurted out on a gasp. He swallowed. His smile was tremulous. "Your Grace, I want—Your Grace, I want—I want *very much* to stay. You—the-the Duchess—his little lordship—why even Lord Vallentine and Madame—pardon the presumption, but I have always considered you all to be my-my—*family*."

The Duke scooped up the documents and the *portefeuille* and got to his feet. "Then it is decided. You will stay, an acknowledged member of my family. The Duchess will be overjoyed."

Finding his legs, Martin Ellicott got to his feet too. "I-I don't —I don't know what to say—How to—How to thank-thank you—"

The Duke held out the documents with a wry smile. "Perhaps you should keep your thanks until you have settled into your new circumstances. And I do not doubt there will be adjustments to make on both sides. Mayhap you will curse me rather than thank me?"

Martin blinked. "I beg your pardon, Your Grace. I don't understand how that could possibly be so."

The Duke gave a huff of laughter. "Of course you don't! Why would you? You've had a lifetime of service, of being gainfully employed. And I have just pulled the metaphorical carpet out from under you by making you a gentleman! You now have to face what we all face, and what is surely the burden carried by most, if not all, of my peers."

"Which is, Your Grace?"

"With no occupation, no need to earn your bread, and with the means to employ others to do even the most menial task, you now have more time on your hands than you will ever know what to do with. How will you fill your days?"

Martin had no idea. It had never crossed his mind because he never expected to ever find himself in this position. The Duke was right. He always had some task to perform, and there had never been enough hours in a day. He was about to comment, when the Duke's attention was diverted by the opening of the door in the bookcase that lead to the private apartments above.

The Duchess stuck her head out of the stairwell into the library.

SPYING THAT the Duke and Martin Ellicott were alone, Antonia returned her husband's smile before disappearing back into the alcove. In the next moment a maid opened the door wider, and out the Duchess stepped, draped in layers of black velvet pinned to a pair of low-cut stays over a thin cotton chemise and black silk under petticoats, all kept together by tacking and a multitude of pins that winked in the candlelight like a hundred tiny points of light.

She tiptoed across the carpet in her stockings, her lady-in-waiting and one of the seamstresses following close at her back, carrying between them what appeared to be a black cloud. They were doing their best to hold up off the floor long folds of trailing velvet, and staying as close as they could possibly manage to the Duchess so the tacking and the pins did not pull free from the material. Both women were so intent on their task that they had no idea they were grimacing under the weight of expectation from the mantua-maker who had threatened their lives if so much as one pin came free from the hours of painstaking work.

To all this Antonia was oblivious, or if she were aware, she did not think it important enough to heed. All that mattered was knowing the outcome of the Duke's interview with Martin.

A lifetime of showing discretion and knowing how to read the moment, Martin had moved off a little way down the library as soon as Antonia had appeared out of the stairwell, which allowed her to speak privately with her husband.

"Before you say it," she announced, falling into the Duke's arms, "I know it! I am undressed and my hair, it is a mess from all the wrapping and unwrapping. I tell you, Renard. I hope this is the only Court presentation I need make in my lifetime! The hoops they are so absurdly wide I have not the first notion of how I am to get into a carriage to travel to the palace. As for climbing down from one…! But me I am certain you have that all worked out. So I will not worry. For now, I had my women remove the hoops because how was I to use the stairs otherwise?" She smiled up at him cheekily and said in a low voice, "I think Mme Claude she is furious with me for leaving in the middle of her pinning. So perhaps you will have to pay her a little more to soothe her temper."

"I will if required. But Mme is more than fairly compensated by having Mme la Duchesse d'Roxton as her client. And once the Court sees you in your fetching gown, she will have many more commissions than she could ever hope to fulfill." His gaze flickered across the section of corset immediately below her deep cleavage. "I presume the décolletage is a little higher when the stomacher is in place, *mignonne*?"

Antonia dropped her chin to inspect her breasts bulging out of the low-cut stays then looked up at him and shrugged. "Mme Claude says it is now the fashion for Court ladies to display their breasts practically naked—"

"Yours will be if you make your curtsey in that!"

Antonia giggled and the Duke winked at her, and then they had the same thought and fell silent on the realisation that they were not now entirely alone. That while they could expect their servants to pretend to deafness when they were playful with each other in the privacy of their apartments, they could not expect the same from their friends and family, and were rightly circumspect when in their company. And while the Duke felt a twinge of awkwardness at this lapse, Antonia's reaction was entirely different because it could only mean one outcome.

She looked across at Martin with a bright expectant smile, and then back up at the Duke. "You have told him, and Martin he has said yes?"

"I did and he has, *ma vie*."

"Bon." She beckoned to Martin, and whispered to the Duke as he came to join them, "But he does not look at all pleased."

"He is beyond pleased. He is stunned. You have turned his world upside down, *ma belle*."

Her green eyes sparkled and she smiled sweetly. "It is a particular talent of mine, is it not?"

The Duke gently kissed her temple. "It is."

Antonia left the Duke's embrace and went to meet Martin when he came up to them, the two women at her back shuffling after her.

"I came as quickly as I could once I knew you had returned from the hotel. How could I wait another moment to see if you and M'sieur le Duc had spoken! But this gown fitting it is very tiring and so here I am half-dressed, for which I apologise because this is an auspicious occasion for all of us, is it not?"

Martin Ellicott stared at her, incapable of uttering a single coherent sentence that could adequately articulate his feelings and the occasion. Overcome, his shoulders shook, and he ran a hand across his mouth before clapping it firmly there for fear he would burst out crying.

Antonia impulsively kissed his cheek. "I am very sure Monseigneur said everything to you that needed to be said, but I want to tell you how happy I am—how happy *you* have made both of us."

Antonia's kiss released Martin from his shock. Smiling shyly, he took hold of the hands she held out to him. "Mme la Duchesse, I do not know how—I can ever tell you—" He glanced at the Duke, before looking into the Duchess's lovely eyes and saying after taking a deep breath, "I will never be able to satisfactorily express the depth of my love and my gratitude to you and to M'sieur le Duc—What it means to me to be embraced as one of the family is-is truly beyond words."

"But, Martin," Antonia replied, "you are my son's godfather, *n'est-ce pas?* After his father and his uncle, there is no better man to offer my son his protection and guidance than you." She kissed one cheek and then the other. "Welcome to the family, *mon très cher ami.*" She then let go of his hands to step back into the circle of the Duke's arm. She smiled up at her husband. "Thank you for making my birthday wish come true, *mon amour.*" And hunching her shoulders with delight and clasping her hands, she declared happily to them both, "Now we will all enjoy ourselves hugely tomorrow!"

SIXTEEN

Antonia's birthday morning began peacefully with the Duke and Duchess partaking of a late breakfast in their apartment. They sipped hot chocolate in bed, their infant son sleeping soundly between them.

The previous night had not been so peaceful. In the early hours, their infant woke in distress, and nothing the Morvan wet nurses or the nursey-maids tried would comfort him. An argument between the wet nurses and the head nursery maid ensued, and sides were taken. The head nursery maid accused one Morvan of consuming too much cabbage at dinner and the other of drinking too much coffee, tainting their breast milk, which in turn gave the noble infant colic. Was it any wonder his little lordship was in distress? Both wet nurses were outraged by such an accusation, and accused the head nursery maid of jealous spite. She, a Parisian, had never approved of the provincial Morvans, and had done everything in her power to make them and their children unwelcome.

Their arguing woke more babies and small children and soon the crying and shouting had the night footmen rushing to the nursery gallery thinking there must be a fire or a break-in, or some such disaster at the very least to cause such a cacophony. And then the housekeeper arrived followed by the butler both in their nightcaps and sleepy-eyed, their concern soon turning to anger.

Finally Lord Vallentine staggered into the center of this nursery melee in nightshirt and Moroccan slippers, nightcap askew. Squinting into the dim light, candlestick held up the better to see, he demanded, then bellowed, for silence. Everyone in the room stopped, except for the babies and small children who continued to wail and whine. Which meant His Lordship was forced to continue to shout to be heard.

He ordered that his screaming nephew be taken to his maman at once. It was obvious the only person who could end this nightmare was Mme la Duchesse. He did not care who woke the ducal couple at three in the morning, but it wasn't going to be him. He then left it to the butler to bring peace to the household, and stomped off, swearing under his breath and murmuring that if his nights of unbroken sleep were numbered, he was going to enjoy every last one of them—asleep.

And now, with the late morning sun streaming across the bedchamber carpet, Antonia sipped her hot chocolate and watched her rosy-cheeked baby son sleeping the sleep of the angels. But she was not thinking of her son or her birthday today but of her birthday the year before. She sighed her contentment.

"At this hour last year, I had already been awake for some time, dressed and waiting for you to return from your ride so you could take me on our excursion. Do you remember?" She took her gaze from her son to give her empty dish to the Duke, and watched him pad across the room and place the tray of chocolate things on the window seat. "We visited a fete and there met a group of elderly Venetian gentlemen."

"I was unaware you were up early and waiting, *ma petite*. But yes, I do remember the fete and the Venetians. We spoke with them in their own language, which greatly impressed them. I know they were all very taken with you, *ma vie*. We had a very pleasant day, did we not?"

"It was the most wonderful birthday I have ever celebrated—until today."

He came back to the bed and smiled down at her. "Then I must make certain today lives up to expectations."

She put out her hand to him and he raised her fingers to kiss.

"But how can today be anything but perfect, when I have you and we have Julian?"

"Perhaps a few more hours of unbroken sleep may have made it better," the Duke quipped, an eye on his heir. "Dare we have him moved do you think?"

Antonia chuckled. "Our regimen it went up the flue last night did it not?"

"It did. And I have it on good authority just who is responsible. It won't happen again… Now I must dress. I have a few matters to attend to before I can spend the rest of the day with you."

THE DUKE WAS SEALING the second of two letters, a footman at his elbow, when a commotion beyond the library door made him pause, ducal seal suspended above a blob of warm red wax. When the double doors remained closed, he pressed his coat of arms into the wax, then set the gold seal aside. He then fluttered the sealed letter like a lady's fan, and satisfied the wax had set, he handed the correspondence to the footman.

"The letter for Lord Shrewsbury is to be delivered by my most trusted courier. The one for Lady Strathsay can be sent in the usual manner."

He waved the footman away, and watched the door close with a self-satisfied smile. In his letter to Edward, Lord Shrewsbury—England's Spymaster General, and an old school friend from their

Eton days—he had all but accused his cousin Augusta Strathsay of being a spy for the French. He mentioned her correspondence with the Comte de Salvan and made vague reference to her regular correspondence with individuals within the French government. That would be enough for Shrewsbury to set his hounds on her! It would ensure that every letter she sent and received would be opened, read, copied, and resealed before it was sent on, delaying her mail considerably.

And she would know her letters were being opened and read by the Spymaster General's office because, in the spirit of fairness and because he wanted her enraged, in his letter to her he told her exactly what he had done.

Served her to rights for meddling in his household, and doing her best to create discord. Now it only remained for him to discover who amongst his servants was in her pay to be her eyes and ears. He was about to ruminate on the possible suspects when the double doors burst open so hard they banged up against the bookcases, jolting him out of his ruminations.

Continuing to sit behind his desk he watched with interest as two footmen under the direction of the porter wrestled to control a young gentleman with a mop of tight black curls who was doing his best to pull himself free without using excessive force. The Duke guessed instantly the stranger's identity but remained impassive and waited for the scene to play out.

The footmen finally brought the young man under control by gripping him hard up under the armpits and lifting him off his feet. And they would have turned about and dragged him from the room but for the Duke's almost imperceptible signal to his porter. With a click of his fingers and one word, the porter had the footmen drop the intruder and step away.

Looking about him and realising he was no longer being detained, the young man brushed down the sleeves of his woolen frockcoat, and tugged at his crumpled cravat, before confidently approaching the desk and making the Duke a magnificent bow.

"I did not mean to bother you, M'sieur le Duc—"

The Duke cut him off.

"You do not—er—bother me, M'sieur Montbelliard. But you have disturbed my household. That fault lies with my incompetent servants, who should've stopped you at the *porte-cochère*. Get out," he snarled at his porter.

Roxton wasn't certain why he permitted anger to get the better of him; perhaps it was lack of sleep after a night spent with a grizzling infant. Or there was the possibility it was because he was none the wiser as to why this young man had decided to haunt his house, and more to the point, was intent on making himself known to his Duchess. He liked having the upper hand in every situation. And this time he did not. He had no idea as to Montbelliard's motivations, if indeed there was anything sinister underlying his actions, and it remained unclear to him if his cousin Salvan was somehow influencing this young man. Both bothered him more than it should. Yet today being Antonia's birthday, it was not the day to speculate on this or anything else. So he would not. He would deal with the deeper mystery another day. For now, he wanted Montbelliard gone, before there was the possibility of his wife meeting him by chance.

He did not offer the young man to sit, and he stayed seated behind his desk.

"I am not at home to visitors. But as you have made it to my library, I will do you the courtesy of allowing you to state your business."

"Thank you, M'sieur le Duc. I wonder if I may have your permission to return on the day that you are home—"

"A question my porter could have answered, rather than you making a nuisance of yourself by forcing your way in here."

"Pardon, M'sieur le Duc, I had no wish to create a disturbance. But your porter he would not listen to my simple request so I—"

"Spare me the petty details," the Duke drawled. "You think

perhaps because we have a—er—familial connection you have right of entry to my house and into my presence?"

"No, M'sieur le Duc. I would not for all the world force myself upon you. And while I am honored to finally make your acquaintance, however brief this interview, it is not you who brought me here on this particular day."

"M'sieur Vallentine is also not at home to guests today."

"The reason I am here is because today is Mme la Duchesse d'Roxton's birthday."

The Duke sat up, astonished. "You know today is my wife's birthday?"

"Yes, M'sieur le Duc." The Chevalier shoved a hand into a deep inner pocket of his frockcoat and after a slight struggle brought out a small package tied up with a satin ribbon. He approached the desk. "I have a small birthday gift for Mme la Duchesse."

The Duke was horrified. He stared at the package as if it were a vial of poison and he told to drink up. "I refuse to receive it! Put it away this instant!"

He knew he was being irrational, that the accompanying sudden hollowness in the pit of his stomach was ludicrous, but for the first time in his life he felt *vulnerable*. It took only a moment to realise from whence such a response had sprung. How many times had he done the same as Montbelliard—shown up at another man's house with a gift for the disconsolate wife—as part of the ritual of seduction.

But he had never been naïve, or stupid, or ill-mannered enough to approach the husband with the gift! His liaisons were always with wives who welcomed his advances. Wives with husbands who were indifferent, and whose marriages were loveless unions for the political and financial benefit of their families. Each party to such an arrangement knew the rules of engagement. But his marriage was something else entirely, something so alien to most of his peers that even now, ten months after he and Antonia had exchanged vows, many were still in shock and disbelief that he had married for one reason and one reason only—for love. It was indubitable.

Surely Montbelliard knew this, or perhaps he thought because M'sieur le Duc was in love with his wife he had lost perspective, and as a consequence lowered his guard? Or maybe someone else —Salvan—had made him think this. Whatever the Chevalier's thoughts and motivations, and whether the Comte de Salvan was implicated or not, Roxton was not prepared to treat him or his gift with anything but contempt.

The Duke stood, and the two footmen came away from the double doors. "M'sieur, this interview is at an end."

The Chevalier seemed to confirm the Duke's original assessment of him when he did not instantly apologise and back away out of his presence with a bow to his knees. He remained where he was, flanked by a liveried footman at each shoulder.

"A thousand apologies, M'sieur le Duc, but Mme de Chavigny asked that I deliver the gift to Mme la Duchess d'Roxton."

At the mention of his aunt by name, the Duke stayed the footmen.

"The gift is—from her?"

"I do not know, M'sieur le Duc."

"So she did not say the gift was from her?"

"She did not, M'sieur le Duc."

"Continue."

"There is little else to tell. When I mentioned to Mme de Chavigny I was returning to Versailles in the hopes of an interview with the masters of *La Grande Écurie*, she asked that I do her this small service—to deliver the package here, to Mme la Duchesse, and on her birthday. It was the least I could do for her many kindnesses to me."

The Chevalier's explanation was plausible, and while it slowed the Duke's heart that the gift was not personally from the Chevalier, it did not quell his suspicion that the Comte de Salvan was somehow involved. After all, Mme de Chavigny was aunt to both him and the Comte, and the ancient martinet was easily swayed. Regardless of the Comte's abhorrent behavior towards Antonia and his subsequent banishment to his estate, he was still head of the Salvan family. And that meant a great deal to the ancient aunts. He knew that if his cousin the Comte said jump, they would do so, and without question.

Roxton also knew with bitter certainty that he presently needed Mme de Chavigny—his *Tante Victoire*—more than she needed him. Court etiquette demanded that only a noblewoman of unimpeachable virtue could sponsor a female wishing to be officially presented to Their Majesties. And the Duke's aunt was one of those rare females, a devout Catholic who had been a devoted wife, and mother of more than a dozen children, two of whom were bishops; another, a nun, was head of a convent school for aristocratic young ladies. And another daughter had the high honor of being lady-in-waiting to the present Queen.

The date for Antonia's Court presentation could not come around quick enough. With that absurd ritual behind them, he and Antonia could get on with their lives, without the interference or approval of his Salvan relatives, from the ancient aunts to this confident stripling standing before him. The young man was possibly telling the truth but there was still something about him that put the Duke on the alert.

"You may inform Mme de Chavigny that you have discharged your duty," he stated, and with a nod to his footmen dismissed the Chevalier by taking up one of the letters on his blotter. "Leave the package on my desk."

"I apologise, M'sieur le Duc, but there—but there is something else. Mme de Chavigny was explicit in her instructions to me about the delivery of the birthday gift." When the Duke lifted his gaze from the letter but said nothing, the Chevalier gulped. "Mme de Chavigny was most forceful in her insistence, and had me give her my word that I would deliver the gift into the hands of Mme la Duchesse d'Roxton in person."

The Duke's reaction was unexpected. He chuckled deep in his throat. Laying aside the letter, he looked across at the Chevalier, all humor extinguished. "You have exposed your ignorance, M'sieur. You are not so well acquainted with Mme de Chavigny as you suppose or you would know that my aunt is never—er—forceful."

"But, M'sieur le Duc, I do not wish to contradict you but Mme de Chavigny she insisted—Yes! Insisted that I deliver this gift in person. She was the one who—"

"*Enough*. Know this: If you ever approach my house or any member of my family again, I will have you sent back from whence you came, never to return. Good day, M'sieur."

The Duke nodded to his footmen. They knew what to do.

The Chevalier looked left and right, eyes widening with panic when he was lifted up by his elbows. He stared at the Duke, who had turned his back and walked over to a wall lined with book-cases. Pulling out a particular book opened the secret stairwell. The Duke left the room via this method, without another word, and without turning around to see if his servants had dispatched his unwanted visitor.

Between them, the footmen dragged the Chevalier backwards out of the library, and out of the villa and unceremoniously dumped him on the cobbles of the avenue. He picked himself up and dusted off his stockings and his breeches. It was only then that he realised he no longer had the birthday gift tied up with a satin ribbon. He swore under his breath. When he had been lifted off his feet, one of the footmen must have snatched it away from him and tossed it across the desk.

THE GIFT FOR THE DUCHESS, with a letter concealed within its wrapping, had left the library in the Duke's pocket.

SEVENTEEN

T HE DUKE and Duchess dressed with exceptional care for Antonia's birthday dinner, wanting to look their best for each other.

Roxton wore an ensemble of black velvet with silver lacings to the cuffs, collar, and flaps to the deep pockets, while his white silk waistcoat was delicately embroidered on front panels and pockets in silver thread and spangles. His knee buckles and the buckles in his black leather shoes were diamond-encrusted. His only jewelry, apart from the ducal emerald ring, was a small, heart-shaped shirt buckle, set with emeralds and diamonds—Antonia's gift for his birthday.

Antonia's *robe à la Française* with matching petticoat was of the palest shell-pink silk with silver thread embroidery. The stomacher and the front panels of the gown were decorated with serpentine ruches, and the tiered *engageantes* at the elbows of her tight-fitting sleeves were of the finest Brussels lace. Her heeled shoes were covered in the same pink silk as her gown, and were also embroidered with silver thread. She wore the emerald and diamond necklace the Duke had given her for her last birthday, and a pair of matching earrings and a bracelet, his gifts to her on their wedding day. Her upswept golden honey hair was plaited, coiled, and threaded with pink silk ribbons, and had pinned in it a delicate feathered aigrette of gold, set with dozens of tiny diamonds—also a gift from her beloved, and presented on the birth of their son.

She chose a painted gouache fan that complemented her gown. And when satisfied with her reflection in the long looking glass in a corner of her dressing closet, she thanked her maids, snatched up the fan, and ran off through the rooms, down the *enfilade* in search of the Duke. But he was not in his rooms. The new valet Geraghty greeted her with the news that she would find M'sieur le Duc awaiting her in the salon off the dining room.

She found him there, standing by the French windows in conversation with Martin Ellicott. Seeing them together brought sudden tears of happiness, which she quickly blinked away before sweeping up to them with a dazzling smile.

"I am sorry to be late, but Gabrielle she could not find the hair brooch," Antonia told them, unconsciously touching the aigrette. She opened wide her eyes and shook her head. "But it was there on the dressing table all the time!" She put her fingers on the Duke's arm, saying to Martin, "How did you spend your first morning of freedom, Martin?"

"Freedom? You imply Martin is a freed slave of the empire, *ma belle*."

Antonia glanced up at him slyly, then said with a sweet smile and a lift of her brows at Martin, "How can Martin be anything else if you are emperor?" When the Duke grinned, she whispered, "You are my Augustus, though I am no Livia—"

"If I am your Augustus, then you are my Livia," the Duke quipped. "And I will bear it as best I can."

Antonia sighed and nodded, appearing disconsolate. "And you may count your good fortune this Livia did not come to our marriage with a cast-off first husband and two ready-made sons for you to worry about."

"Such impediments did not stop Augustus, and they certainly wouldn't have stopped me," the Duke retorted, adding with a soft smile down at her, "I'd have married you regardless, *ma vie*."

"That makes me very happy! But I am also glad not to have a cast-off first husband because me I do not like the idea of making anyone sad. And he would have been very sad, would he not? Imagine living with the knowledge that as soon as his wife—*me*—she saw *you*, she never gave him another thought! That is what happened with Livia and Augustus."

The Duke laughed out loud and so did Martin, so much to the latter's great surprise that he clapped a hand to his mouth. Antonia leaned in to Martin, saying with a light in her eyes, "I am sorry but you will have to bear with our silliness. We do not stand on ceremony with family. Is that not so, Monseigneur?"

"I believe Martin has been well aware of our—er—silliness for some time now, *ma fée*. And is most expert in knowing when to—er—close his ears and his eyes." When Antonia's eyes widened and she mouthed "oh", he winked at her. "Just so, *mignonne*."

"This timing of Monseigneur making you a gentleman of means could not have been better timed," Antonia remarked confidentially to Martin. "Because last night Julian he was brought to us in the middle of the night, and in such distress that his screaming it woke all our servants. Monseigneur's first thought was the house, it was ablaze! I do not remember the half of it because all I was thinking about was *mon pauvre petit garçon*. But Monseigneur he tells me everyone was wild-eyed and trembling in their half-waking, half-dressed states that it was comical. And poor Juju he would not stop his crying. And then, just as I was at my wits' end, Monseigneur he had the most excellent idea that I sing to our son. And so that is what I did, and in Italian."

"And did that help, Mme la Duchesse?" Martin asked politely, a glance at the Duke who had taken his gaze to the ceiling.

Antonia saw the look and giggled. "No. But I think it helped to distract his exasperated papa."

"You have a lovely singing voice, *ma vie*. I have always said so."

"I do when you can hear it!" Antonia retorted. "But it helped me too. To sing. Because it distracted me a little. And then, the problem it fixed itself, and Julian he stopped his crying." She snapped her fingers. "Just like that."

"How, Mme la Duchesse?" Martin asked, genuinely intrigued.

"What is of infinitely more interest," drawled the Duke, hoping to turn the conversation, "is the answer to the question you asked Martin earlier about how he spent his first morning of —er—freedom."

Antonia and Martin ignored him.

"It happened while Monseigneur he was pacing up and down our bedchamber with Julian at his shoulder," Antonia confided in Martin. She cocked her head in thought, the closed sticks of her fan to her chin. "I think it was having him upright, and the movement of the walking and the rubbing of his back, all these combined made it happen." She caught at Martin's sleeve and said with a smile of breathless awe, "My son he did the loudest belch I have ever heard in my life! It is true I tell you. I would not have thought it possible that such a tiny being could produce such a noise, if I had not heard it with my own ears, but he did!"

"Martin may not have any experience of infants, *mignonne*, but one does not need to, to know that they are capable of the most-the most—er—*startling* emissions. And I do not doubt that in time, if Martin is fortunate, he will be privy to all sorts of our son's most remarkable developments. And be just as fascinated by them as we are."

"You can count on it, Your Grace," Martin replied with all the dignity he could muster, while trying to suppress a chuckle at the sight in his mind's eye of this most austere nobleman with a belching infant at his shoulder.

The Duke inclined his head and mouthed "thank you", then signaled for a footman with a tray to come forward and present them with glasses of champagne. These were eagerly taken up, the Duke proposing a toast.

"We will have the formal birthday toast when we dine," the Duke said. "But I could not let the opportunity pass for the three of us to raise our glasses, and to you, Martin."

"Thank you, Your Grace," Martin replied diffidently. "I confess I am still in a state of shock—"

"And you not the only one!" quipped the Duke.

"You refer to the household, Your Grace?" asked Martin. "I own it was strange to venture beyond the green door to say my farewells, but it was made easier by circumstance. Everyone was preoccupied in preparing for today's celebration that I did not want to disturb such industriousness. And no one was more so than Jean-Camille who with the help of several kitchen staff was boxing up the dozens of macarons to send on to the hotel—"

"Monseigneur, you had macarons sent to Paris?" Antonia interrupted in wonder. "For all the household?"

"I did. I thought it would make for a nice gesture if not only my sister, but our entire household at the hotel, and here, were to receive macarons in honor of your birthday." The Duke sipped from his glass, well pleased with himself. "I cannot take credit for the initial idea, but I will own to have inaugurated the yearly tradition of distributing macarons amongst my servants and family in celebration of Mme la Duchesse d'Roxton's birthday—"

"Oh, I like this idea of a tradition very much!" Antonia declared, clapping her hands with delight. "You have made the day doubly delightful, Monseigneur! Thank you. It is as if I have been granted two wishes, when all I asked for was the one. But please, Martin, what did you do this morning in your very own apartment?"

"I can't imagine you were able to remain asleep to fill in a couple of hours," quipped the Duke.

"After two decades of rising with the sun, Your Grace?" Martin shook his head. "But it did give me time to write several letters

before breakfast and my appointment with the tailor… I wrote to
—I wrote—excuse me…"

When he took a moment to sip his champagne, a sudden
constriction in his throat and tears behind his eyes, the Duke and
Duchess exchanged an understanding smile. To fill an awkward
silence she did not want Martin to feel in the least, Antonia was
about to ask the Duke the whereabouts of Lord Vallentine, who
was surely late for the celebrations, when Martin found his voice
and continued.

"The first person I wrote to was my mother."

The Duke was taken aback. "Mrs. Ellicott is—" He was about
to say alive but quickly modified this. "She is well?"

"She is very well indeed, Your Grace," Martin responded with
a smile. "She lives at one end of your village of Alston, in a
pleasant house overlooking the river."

"It belongs to Monseigneur this house?" Antonia asked.

"The entire village belongs to me, *ma belle*," the Duke drawled.
He frowned and asked Martin, "I have a vague recollection of Ellicott coming to me about the state of those houses…"

"My father approached Your Grace not long after the death of
the fourth duke because the situation was dire. He informed you
of the sad neglect to the village and many of the tenant houses. I
am sure you do not remember his request, particularly as we—you
and Lord Vallentine, and myself and several other servants, were
preoccupied with organising for our departure for the Italian States
and the Greek islands."

"And Monseigneur he of course had all the houses repaired,"
Antonia stated confidently.

"He did, Mme la Duchesse," Martin confirmed. "Inside and
out, providing each with a new roof and chimney. And the village
bridge was rebuilt so those on the left bank could cross with ease
without having to make the two-mile journey to the stepping-
stone bridge at the weir."

Antonia smiled up at the Duke knowingly. "Did not my father

say your blackened shell covered a multitude of decencies?! *En voici la preuve!*"

"Your unswerving belief in me is a reassuring and a—er—constant delight, *chère épouse*," the Duke responded with a self-effacing smile. "But I believe—particularly in relation to the village of Alston—that if I did indeed have all the houses repaired and the bridge rebuilt, I would have done so not for purely altruistic reasons. I would have reacted rather than acted, all because it was the last thing my grandfather would have wished. He was a tyrannical penny pincher." Roxton raised his glass and grinned. "Which I am daily grateful for, because he left me an enormous fortune—"

"Which you have used to help others," Antonia stated firmly. "And do not say otherwise because me I know it to be so!" She said to Martin before the Duke could respond, "When we return to Treat, I would very much like to make your mother's acquaintance. I will come to her. If that is agreeable?"

"She would be honored, Mme la Duchesse. Perhaps we can—we can go together…?"

"Yes! That is a wonderful idea, Martin."

The Duke set his jaw and put up his chin. "Do not think I am unaware of what is going on here between the two of you! No sooner will you sit down to tea and cake than you'll be making enquiries of Mrs. Ellicott about me as a boy—no! Do not try and deny it!"

Antonia looked up at him with wide innocent eyes. "But, Monseigneur. I was not about to do anything of the sort. That is exactly what I mean to do."

The Duke and Martin Ellicott looked at her, looked at one another, and burst out laughing. It was just as Lord Vallentine sauntered into the salon. But what caused the laughter to die and astonishment to be writ large on the faces of the Duchess and Martin Ellicott was that Vallentine was holding the Duke and Duchess's pride and joy. The Duke, however, was not entirely surprised. He put up his quizzing glass to stare at his best friend from shoe buckles to powdered wig with a well-satisfied smile. His orders had been carried out to the letter.

Behind His Lordship trailed a gaggle of nursey-maids and footmen carrying various infant paraphernalia. And as Lord Vallentine came across the room, this gaggle went through into the dining room to offload the wicker baby basket, blankets, cushions, baby clothing, and bibs, and an assortment of rattles, two of the most experienced nurserymaids remaining behind to be of assistance with the ducal infant during dinner, if and when required.

Lord Vallentine had not taken more than a few steps across the carpet when Antonia rushed up to him in a rustle of silk, full of smiles and all for her infant, whose little face split into a grin upon seeing his mother's beloved face. She spoke to him in the voice she used for him exclusively, tickling him under his chubby chin, planting kisses on his fist, and asking if he had been on his best behavior for *ton oncle et parrain.*

Lord Vallentine was all for handing over his nephew, but as Antonia still held her champagne glass, and the Duke had sauntered up to him but did not offer to take his son either, he continued to hold the ducal bundle of joy, announcing with satisfaction,

"He's been watered, washed, and wrapped up. And for a second time because he had already been washed and dressed when there was a mishap. So he is wearing his second-best smock. And what a procedure! Damme!" He rolled his eyes and huffed. "Never knew so much could come up and out of one so tiny, and at speed, too!"

"And now you do," the Duke teased.

"My poor darling boy. I hope now your belly it is more settled," Antonia said to her infant before glancing suspiciously from her brother-in-law to her husband and back again. "I am very happy to see you have spent time with our son, Lucian, but why were you discovering these things on this of all days?"

When she pressed her champagne glass on the Duke to take her son, Vallentine handed him over, saying casually without answering her question, "I was instructed to assure you both that his little lordship is wearing padding and a triple clout under his woolen pilch. Whatever the heck that all means! But I'm sure you do, and will be pleased. The head nursery maid said you would be."

Antonia nuzzled her son before lifting him above her with wide eyes and a big smile, which made him squeal with delight. "It means we should have no little accidents during our meal and his maman's birthday gown will remain dry." She brought him down to sit him on her hip and looked across at Vallentine. "But I still do not understand your sudden interest in such details that I am very sure you, like Monseigneur, prefer to leave to those who are— as Monseigneur says—most expert."

"I do not doubt Vallentine's time in the nursery was—er— instructive in many ways, *ma vie*," offered the Duke, still with that teasing tone which put Antonia on the alert. "And that he now has a vivid appreciation of the regimen we are doing our best to effect so that our son and ourselves can live a more—er—harmonious existence."

"Do I! I learned a thing or two about infants, and more than I ever wanted to know," Vallentine revealed and pulled a face which made Antonia giggle. He looked askance at his best friend. "And you don't have to instruct me twice. Your message was delivered as loud and as clear as the bells of the *Paroisse Notre- Dame*." He snatched up a glass of champagne being offered to him by a hovering footman and threw back half the liquid before adding with a heavy sigh, pointing the glass at the Duke, "It's given me the perfect excuse to have it out with Estée about our own—what did you call it?—regimen! I'll be leavin' the precious infant to who is most expert at three in the mornin', I can tell you!"

"I'm pleased to hear it," replied the Duke. "And that your visit to the nursery gallery provided you with a better appreciation of the need for unbroken sleep."

Antonia suddenly understood and she stepped up to Vallentine with a scowl. "So it was you who upset Julian in the early hours!"

"*Me?* Up—upset *him?*" Vallentine repeated in a thin voice of incredulousness. "He was howlin' the place down well before I got to the nursery to sort matters to rights."

"But you did not sort it, did you, Lucian?" Antonia replied. "And I see now why you spent the morning in the nursery, not because you wanted to but because Monseigneur he sent you there as a penance. But no matter, *mon petit homme chéri,*" she cooed to her infant. "It is as well you have two godfathers, for I know the other one he does genuinely care about you—"

"Hey! Now that ain't fair," Vallentine grumbled.

"It is too late to pretend an interest in my son," Antonia interrupted teasingly, and turned about when the double doors into the dining room were thrown wide by two footmen, and the butler stepped forward to announce dinner was ready.

Antonia took one sweeping look into the flower-filled dining room and gasped. There were colorful blooms in tubs around the walls just as there were in the salon, but what opened her eyes wider was the dining table decorated with silver, crystal, and porcelain, and delicate, colorful flower pastilles in woven baskets. And all under a blaze of twinkling candlelight, with a liveried footman behind each chair, and the nursery maids by the ornate cradle. She turned back to the Duke with a teary smile.

"Oh, Renard! It is—*Il est parfait!* *This* is the best birthday!" And to her son, she whispered at his ear, "And you, *mon ange,* have the best papa in all the world."

EIGHTEEN

"Y‌ou've fashioned a rod for your own back, y'know that, don't you?" Vallentine quipped to the Duke as they followed Antonia into the decorated dining room. "Next year she'll be expectin' an even more elaborate arrangement for the occasion, with even more blooms and baubles, and who knows what else! Ha! Ha!"

"Are you implying I am incapable of providing for my wife and her happiness, Lucian?" Roxton drawled, well-pleased his instructions had been carried out to the letter, and that Antonia was suitably surprised and delighted.

Lord Vallentine was too tired to care if his friend was being flippant or not, though he guessed the former. He threw up a hand.

"Damme! Don't you start on me too! I've had a shatterin' morning, thanks to you. Instructive but shatterin', and what I need now is a glass of your best claret and—"

He gave a start and stopped dead before reaching his chair.

The Duke took his place at the head of the table. Antonia was at its foot, settling her son into his cradle with the help of the nursery maids. The ducal infant was propped up with pillows so that he was supported and secure, with a good view of proceedings, particularly his mother, his cradle within arm's reach. He was given a rattle, and this he gripped and waved about, making the little silver bells tinkle, gurgling his delight in response.

But it was the fourth diner that had Lord Vallentine's shoes stuck to the parquetry. Martin Ellicott took his cue from the Duke and sat to his left hand, directly opposite the seat to be occupied by Lord Vallentine. It was an intimate arrangement, with the diners in close proximity so conversation could be heard by all. The multitude of dishes on offer could easily be passed around without the need for servant interference, although footmen would have to come and go with dishes because not all could be served at once, which was the usual custom, due to the reduced size of the table.

If His Lordship had noticed Martin Ellicott standing at the Duke's elbow in the salon it was not worth commenting upon. After all, the valet did appear at his master's side upon occasion, and it just wasn't done to acknowledge a servant, unless necessary or called upon to do so. And so he had thought nothing of Ellicott's presence. The Duke obviously had his reasons for his valet being there that were none of his concern. But now, as they moved into the dining room, so too had the valet, and not only had he taken his place at the table—in the seat which would have been occupied by His Lordship's wife had she been well enough to be there—he was having his glass filled by a footman and a folded napkin placed across his left knee, as if he had every right to sit at the table of his master.

Lord Vallentine could not fathom it and he decided the joke was on him. He hastily went to his place and plonked down, dragging the napkin across his silken knees before resting his elbows on the table and taking up his glass, which was now filled with claret. He put up his chin, a sidelong look at Martin Ellicott before demanding of the Duke,

"All right. I took m'punishment for not followin' the expert advice of your nursery maids and foistin' your screaming infant on you at three in the morning, but this has me dumbfounded. What's the prank, eh?"

"I beg your pardon, Lucian. Prank?"

Vallentine opened wide his eyes and jerked his head in direction of Martin Ellicott, who had turned in response to something the Duchess had said, now she had taken her seat at the table. "This," he whispered loudly. "That's Estée's place. And you-know-who is sittin' in it!"

"It is. When my sister is here. But she is not. And when she is again, the chairs will be—er—rearranged accordingly."

"You know that's not what I meant!" His Lordship blustered in a loud hissed aside. He sat up and clicked his tongue. "All right. Have it your way. Damme. I'll go along with whatever this is, because I suspect it's not your doin' so you're not to blame. It is her birthday after all."

"There is no blame, Vallentine," Antonia interrupted.

She had overheard, and knew the moment something was not quite right at her table when Martin dropped his chin and lowered his eyes to his plate. He too had heard. She looked across at the Duke and when he smiled at her encouragingly, she returned his smile and continued.

"I have at my birthday celebration the people who mean the most to me in all the world. If Madame had been well enough to attend, then the dinner it would have been perfect. But all the men are here: My husband, my son, my brother-in-law and my son's uncle, and my son's godfathers—they who also happen to be our closest friends." She turned to Martin and said sweetly, "I do not believe you have been formally introduced to His Lordship, Martin. Lord Vallentine is M'sieur le Duc's best friend, and he is the husband of my sister-in-law, Monseigneur's sister. He is also my son's uncle, and his godfather, like you. He is the greatest swordsman in all France and England, so he is very brave and fearless. And Lucian," she continued, turning to address Lord Vallentine, "I wish you to be known to M'sieur Ellicott, a gentleman of independent means who is also my son's godfather, and a great friend of M'sieur le Duc. They have known each other since they were boys." She glanced at Martin, tears in her eyes. "Martin he saved my life and the life of my son, and so is also brave and fearless. In that you have much in common… It is a wish of mine, and also of Monseigneur, that you will become good friends."

There were a few seconds of silence and then Martin pushed back his chair and rose to his feet. He bowed to Vallentine, but it was not a bow of subservience, but one of politeness, as when two strangers on the same footing greet each other in the street. And then Lord Vallentine set aside his napkin and rose up. He looked directly at Martin, and then he too bowed, and in the same manner, as a man meeting a stranger he takes for his peer. And then he did something more, something which cemented his affection with his hosts, and set everyone at their ease. He stuck out his hand across the table.

"Honored to make your acquaintance, M'sieur."

"The honor is mine, my lord," Martin replied.

They shook hands, resumed their seats and once again put their napkins across their laps.

Antonia could not have wished for a better outcome to make her birthday that much more special. But then the Duke surprised her. He signaled to a footman, who came across and set before the Duchess a silver tray that had upon it several wrapped packages tied up with different-colored ribbons. Antonia stared at the Duke.

"For me? But you have already granted my birthday wish, Monseigneur!"

"Who else has a birthday today, aye?" Lord Vallentine declared, eyes rolling to the plastered ceiling, before he leaned in and stabbed his finger at the silver tray. "And no shakin' 'em about like you did last year! You're a duchess now and need to show some decor—"

"As a duchess I can tell you, Vallentine, to stop being old in the head, as you always are!" Antonia picked up one of the packages and showed it to her son. "What do you think is in this parcel for your maman, Juju?"

"He can't tell you!" Vallentine declared on a scoff.

Antonia ignored His Lordship and said to the Duke, "Perhaps we should eat first and I will open my gifts with the coffee and cake."

"If that is your wish."

"No! Not this year!" Vallentine declared stubbornly. "I'm not havin' it. Besides, there's one gift in particular I do know about, so perhaps we can start with that one."

"As much as I would like to say I am gratifying Lucian's impatience," said the Duke, "I own to wanting to satisfy my own. Would you do us all the kindness of looking over your shoulder to the fireplace, *mignonne*."

Antonia did as she was asked, and what she saw had her hands to her cheeks.

Footmen had carefully removed the tubs of flowers, the folding screen, and a large linen sheet, to reveal a most magnificent sedan chair. All four sides of this personal traveling conveyance were painted with bright pastoral scenes on a gold background, and were varnished to a high sheen with *vernis Martin*. The three window panels were bordered with gilded woodwork of acanthus leaves and bouquets of flowers, and on the door and the back panel were painted the Roxton ducal coat of arms. And all under a domed roof of brass-studded panels of stretched black leather that had at its apex a ducal coronet in gilded wood.

She glanced back at the Duke. "It is mine?"

"I could not have my duchess transported about Versailles in anything less than her own chair."

"I have seen the great ladies taken about the corridors of the palace and out into the gardens in their beautiful chairs, but never did I expect to have one of my very own! And this one, it is *magnifique*."

"As it should be for Mme la Duchesse d'Roxton." When she hesitated, the Duke smiled. "Please. You must take a closer look. Vallentine's hunger pangs will wait."

Antonia dashed over to the fireplace and skipped about the chair, inspecting all four sides. She peered in through the windows and then opened the door. And when she stuck her head inside, she discovered an opulent interior. There was a bench with side arms, the whole covered in a padded wool velvet with floral motifs. The walls and ceiling were lined in a matching pattern, while the curtains to the three windows were made of a gold silk damask. By the padded bench, under the right-hand side window and set in a niche, was a small gold carriage clock. And under the left-hand side window, was a pocket for small necessary items, such as a lady's fan, her prayer book, and a hand mirror.

The sedan chair was a superb piece of craftsmanship that had no equal. Yet, what would open wide the eyes of the heads that turned as this elegant traveling chair passed them by were its two beefy chairmen in their liveried uniforms. They stood as sentries to one side of the fireplace, a shiny leather and brass harness fitted over their wide shoulders, and holding in a large gloved hand a very long polished, painted wooden pole, that when slotted into the respective brackets of the sedan chair, were used to lift up the chair between them and carry its occupant wherever she wished to go.

Antonia could not resist bunching up her silk petticoats, climbing inside the chair, and closing the door. She sat on the padded bench and looked about her in wonder. And then she pulled down the window sash and peered out, beaming with happiness.

"There is room enough for Julian to sit upon my lap and look out!"

"If you're goin' to take the ducal infant up with you, then it's a pity there ain't room enough for one of the nursery maids as well," quipped Lord Vallentine. "I'd not be leavin' home without at least one of 'em, preferably two."

"That conveyance is known as a carriage, Lucian," drawled the Duke, and signaled to the two chairmen to take themselves off. He asked Antonia in a different voice, "Shall we commence eating without you, *ma belle?*"

"Oh yes! I am too excited and happy to eat," she announced from the sedan chair window, and spent a few moments longer inspecting the opulent interior.

"Those two look as if they could lift a carriage!" Vallentine remarked, watching the chairmen depart, taking the chair poles with them. He added in an under voice to the Duke, "Good to see you'll have her well-protected when she goes out and about without you."

"They have their orders, and my blessing to do what is necessary."

"You think—Pardon, Your Grace," Martin said in English, and in the same under voice, following their lead and doing his best to temper his concern. "Surely there is no immediate threat—?"

"If you mean from my cousin rusticating in Limoges—no, but—"

"You can never be too careful! Damme!" Vallentine interrupted, grinding his teeth. "And until that worm is cold in the ground with his fellow worms, we all need to keep vigilant."

"Of course, my lord," Martin agreed. "I will—"

"Time to talk later!" hissed Lord Vallentine, grabbing for the closest covered dish and pretending an interest in its contents, because Antonia had emerged from her sedan chair and was closing the door.

She ran up to the Duke, who had set down his silver knife and fork. "Thank you!" she said, kissing his cheek. "You are too good to me as always. You spoil me."

"It is my prerogative to spoil you. It pleases me to give you these small tokens, *ma fée*, just as much as it does you to receive them. So the pleasure it is also mine. You understand?" When she nodded, he squeezed her fingers and said softly, "Perhaps you should eat too?"

"I will, and open the little packages while I do."

And as the gentlemen passed dishes amongst themselves, beginning with four types of soup, and going on to pile their plates with a variety of roast meats and vegetable delicacies, Antonia enjoyed a bowl of cream of chicken soup, and then ate sparingly of a few of the various courses on offer. And in between these courses, she unwrapped her gifts. She gave the discarded wrapping and ribbon to her son to play with. And when she opened each box, she took great delight in showing her infant the contents first before sharing it with the rest of the diners.

Madame and Vallentine had gifted her a painted porcelain bonbonniere in the shape of a whippet curled up asleep. A fine gold chain attached to the hinged lid ended in a small clip which allowed the bonbonniere to be affixed to Antonia's necessarie. To Vallentine she blew a kiss of thanks, and he responded by waving his fork about.

The second box contained a bookmark made of silk and velvet. It was embroidered with a delicate spray of flowers trailing down its length, and ended in a fringe. In its center were the intertwined initials A and R, finely stitched within an oval frame. There was a small note in the box that read simply 'from M.E.'.

"Thank you, Martin. I shall treasure this and use it every day. It is even more special because you made this yourself, yes?"

"I did, Mme la Duchesse." His smile was shy. "I think you discovered my pastime on our crossing to England, did you not?"

"And then I made you tell me all about it. He is a master of the stitch, Monseigneur," she stated proudly and gave the book-mark in its box to Martin to show the Duke. "Martin's mother was his teacher."

"She was of the strong belief that to excel in one's vocation, one needs to be expert in many fields, stitchery being one of them," Martin explained, passing the box to the Duke. "Embroidery was simply an extension of that skill and something I enjoy when time is my own."

"Most impressive," complimented the Duke, appraising the work through his quizzing glass. "I see you will be suitably occupied in the evenings, should you not care to play at cards, or you find the conversation or the entertainment on offer insipid."

"Never insipid, Your Grace."

"Perhaps you'll have more success than my wife at coaxin' the Duchess to learn how to use a tambour," Vallentine commented, knowing he was goading Antonia, and with a distracted eye on the footmen who were coming and going, replacing the empty uncovered dishes with new courses.

"But why should I learn how to use a tambour when now we have two expert embroiderers in the family? And do not tell me I need to know how to use it for when M'sieur le Duc and I we have a daughter, because I can now call on Martin or Madame to show her how to become expert with her needle. So this problem it solves itself."

"It would be an honor, Mme la Duchesse," Martin stated.

"Now don't you take her side against me, too!" Lord Vallentine complained good-naturedly as he reached for the closest covered dish. "I'm already on the back foot as it is, with Roxton and m'wife refusin' to take sides. And I can never win with her, y'know. She has this way of twistin' m'words—"

"Because they do not take sides, does not mean they are on my side, Lucian," Antonia interrupted, sitting her infant son on her lap on the cushion the nursery maid had placed there. She looked across at the Duke with a cheeky smile, before saying to Vallentine, "It only means that they are not on yours."

"See what *I* mean," Vallentine grumbled to Martin. He lifted the lid off a dish and his eyes lit up to find *truite à l'ail et sauce aux amandes*. He heaped a serving on his plate and then offered the dish to Martin. "Try this," he urged, and shot a look at Antonia. But as she seemed preoccupied with her infant, he added confidentially and with a wink, "The garlic and almond sauce is delicious with the trout, but not somethin' I can eat when the lady wife is about."

"Perhaps that is because it is full of almonds, and just like the *Nougat de Montélimar*, which you should also not eat, it gives you excessive wind," Antonia stated matter-of-factly, as she reached for the third gift and the note that came with it. But muffled chuckles and a splutter made her glance up to find Lord Vallentine shaking his head and mumbling incoherently, and the Duke and Martin with their napkins pressed to their mouths. "But—Lucian, it must be the almonds, *n'est-ce pas*. So I do not understand at all why you continue to eat them." Baffled, she looked to the Duke for confirmation. "If he eats almonds, it gives him the wind. Madame she complains of it, and says that Lucian he still insists on eating them, even though they do not agree with him. Is there something wrong with my warning, Monseigneur?"

The Duke removed his napkin and schooled his features into a look of polite concern. "I do not think Lucian is unaware of the problem, *ma vie*. It's just that it embarrasses him to have you address his—er—unfortunate condition so-so—*directly*."

Antonia threw up a hand, mystified. "But Madame does so all the time, and at table. And if Lucian had not mentioned it just now, I would not have done so either."

"I didn't mention—Oh, all right! Damme!" Vallentine conceded when Antonia opened wide her eyes. "I alluded to it, but I didn't say it." Adding in an embarrassed grumble, "And Estée might warn me at table, but she don't do so in mixed company."

"But there is no mixed company here, Lucian," Antonia stated firmly. She kissed the top of her son's white cap before smiling across at the Duke, adding softly, "Here there is only family."

"If His Majesty must bear with having his every bodily function reported to the world, Lucian, then you can bear with having a wife and a sister who are concerned for your health," remarked the Duke, taking up his wine glass, a wink at the Duchess. "To see it any other way would be to complain about what is nothing more than a puff of—er—as we are being blunt—hot air…" And to change the subject, and because he was curious about the gift from Mme de Chavigny, the Chevalier Montbelliard had been most insistent he present to Antonia in person, he asked, "Is that the gift from *Tante Victoire, ma belle?*"

She nodded and looked up, distracted by the note found in the wrapping. "Three lovely lace-bordered handkerchiefs embroidered with my initial."

"Handkerchiefs? Our son certainly approves," the Duke replied with a grin, watching his infant playing tug of war with one of the handkerchiefs that he had in both fists. "Care to share her birthday wishes?" he asked lightly, sipping at his wine.

Antonia did not hesitate to relate the contents of the note.

"It is curious that it is not in her hand, but perhaps she had her lady-in-waiting write it for her, because her arthritis it is very bad at this time of year. She wishes me a very happy day with you and our son… and is looking forward to seeing us, but most particularly seeing how much Julian he has grown."

When Antonia folded the note and put it in the box with two of the handkerchiefs, and then slid it out of reach of their infant, the Duke persisted with his questioning, knowing that there must be more to the note than she had revealed, and was possibly wanting to shield him from the consequences.

"Did she make mention of when we can expect her? She assured me she would be here with plenty of time to spare before your Court presentation."

Antonia met his dark eyes and said, letting out a small sigh of resignation, "I do not know why I try to keep things from you, because you know it anyway! And as you have now asked, I will tell you. But I did not want to spoil our day because I know you will not be pleased with her. *Tante Victoire* she says it is not her fault, but to avoid a family squabble she cannot now stay with us."

The Duke smiled crookedly. "*Tante Victoire* was ever—er—persuadable."

"Persuadable?" Vallentine huffed. "You could puff on that ancient aunt and she'd blow her opinions over to the other side!"

"You had best read her excuses for yourself," Antonia said as she passed Mme de Chavigny's note to Martin to give to the Duke.

Roxton perused the note through his quizzing glass. And while he did, the rest of the diners finished what was left on their plates, and drank what remained of their wine. But Antonia could see the Duke was far from pleased and was doing his best not to show it, so she said brightly, to break the silence,

"Whichever relative *Tante Victorie* chooses to stay with—sister or niece—it will give me the perfect opportunity to visit them in my beautiful new birthday chair, yes?"

At that the Duke allowed the storm of his displeasure with his Salvan relatives to pass. He would deal with them tomorrow. He lifted his glass and returned Antonia's smile. "It will that, *ma belle.*"

"As I see it, *Tante Victoire* has made some poor choices in her day, but incurring your displeasure has to be at the top her list of poor choices!" Vallentine chuckled, as he nibbled on a garlic-soaked partridge wing. He pointed the tiny bone at the Duke. "If I were inclined to wager, I'd say the fact you need her for this presentation has emboldened her to act rashly in some way, or in some endeavour."

"How perceptive of you, Lucian. You may well be right, or her sister and niece are using the squabble and *Tante Victoire* to tie my —er—hands because they want something from *me.*"

"But if they want something from you, Monseigneur," Antonia argued. "Why do they not just come out and ask you? And then they will have their answer."

"They're scared," stated Vallentine. "Of the answer and of your husband—"

"That is ridiculous!" Antonia stated hotly. "What is there to be scared of when Monseigneur his response will always be a fair one."

The Duke inclined his head with a smile. "Thank you, *ma vie*." He folded the note and gave it to Martin to return to Antonia, who slipped it back in the box with the handkerchiefs. And to Lord Vallentine he said cryptically, "When you think of the question, Lucian, there is your answer."

His Lordship had no idea what his best friend meant but he had an inkling it had everything to do with the Salvan women championing the cause of the Chevalier Montbelliard. So he let drop any further questions on the topic, but one. "So which silly sister and which hare-brained niece does *Tante Victoire* have to choose between for her stay here in Versailles, because there are at least half a dozen of both."

"*Tante Philippe* is—er—squabbling with her daughter-in-law Marie-Louise, Duchesse du Touraine—"

"*What?* Philippe the Pious?" Lord Vallentine blurted out. He pulled a face of disgust. "And Touraine the Terror? A nursery full of screamin' smelly brats is preferable to one hour in the company of either of those two dismal dames. And I should know! I went twice with Estée to visit *Tante Victoire. Tante Philippe* and Mme Touraine were both there, and they were *all* squabblin'! Don't ask me about what, damme, but Estée soon joined in the fray. I took myself off to admire the shrubbery."

"You went twice?" The Duke lips twitched and he put up his brows. "I had no idea courting my sister had been such a trial for you."

"Trial?" Vallentine rolled his eyes. "You have no idea!" He blew out his lips and shook his head. "I'd rather stay in a ditch, than with any of that lot!"

Everyone at the table laughed, and then Antonia gasped and stared at Vallentine as if shocked beyond measure.

"Oh no you don't!" His Lordship complained. "You can't chastise me for voicin' what we *all* think of *Tante Philippe* and Mme Touraine—"

"No! No! I do not care in the least what you say about *them*. It is all true. No. What I want, Lucian, is for you to do what you just did again. *S'il vous plaît.*"

His Lordship frowned. "Do wh—"

"That silly noise you made with your lips."

"But, why would—"

"Renard! Did you see?" Antonia asked, eyes bright with excitement. "Did you hear?"

The Duke had not, but he had an inkling her delight had everything to do with their infant, who had turned his head at the sound of his mother's voice and was looking up at her. "Lucian, oblige the Duchess, if you would be so kind."

"Very well. But all I did was blow out my lips like this."

Vallentine did it again, and was about to comment as to why it was necessary to descend to the antics of a fool when he too gave a start at an unfamiliar sound. He stared first at Antonia, and then at the Duke, and finally at Martin. Everyone else had heard it too, because they were all momentarily stunned.

His little lordship, Julian Renard Hesham, Marquis of Alston and heir to the Roxton dukedom, had marked another momentous stage in his development by producing his first giggle. He had been looking up at his mother, but the moment Lord Vallentine blew out his lips again, he turned his head to look straight at the source of such a strange noise. Lord Vallentine blew out his lips a third time, as if to assure himself and the rest of the diners that this was the source of his little lordship's giggles. And sure enough, the ducal infant giggled, and he kept giggling. It was such an infectious little gurgle of happiness that it had everyone grinning.

Although, when he thought about it later that night while

dressing for bed, Vallentine wondered, and not for the first time, if much of that laughter was not only in response to his nephew's new-found ability to giggle, but was directed at him. For having obliged Antonia by blowing out his lips to get her son to giggle all the more, he added pulling faces to his repertoire. It amazed him to what lengths grown adults descended to amuse the very young.

But in the end, it mattered not. Everyone had enjoyed the Duchess's birthday dinner immensely. Although he regretted being stubborn and not listening to her advice. He wished he had possessed the resolve to forgo the trout with the almond sauce, because he spent most of the night feeling bloated and queasy. It gave him a new-found appreciation for his nephew's pangs of belly pain. Still. He'd never let on to Antonia. And he'd indulge again. But not tomorrow, or the next day. Perhaps he'd give almonds and the *Nougat de Montélimar* a miss for the next month. And with that decision made, Vallentine was finally able to drift off to sleep, hoping he slept right through until late morning. He knew his days of unbroken sleep were numbered—he had five months, and he was counting down until his own bundle of joy arrived. He couldn't wait!

BEHIND-THE-SCENES

Explore the real people, places, objects, and
history in *His Duchess* on Pinterest.
www.pinterest.com.au/lucindabrant/roxton-foundation-series.